# JUDAS

Indignant Few MC Book 1

DEJA VOSS

# 1

## Judas: 25 Years Ago - Age 7

I held the fabric in my fingers, tugging at the stretchy dress, holding it to my nose, rubbing it on my face, smearing away the stinging tears in my eyes.

I wasn't a baby. I was way too old to be hiding in Mama's closet, watching the world go by through the slats in the wooden doors. Watching as the aunts and uncles I never really knew taped up brown boxes of Mama and Daddy's stuff. This tiny little room was the only place I could breathe. Breathe the smell of my mama's perfume on that dress she only wore to church on Christmas when we had to get fancy for Jesus's people. The smell of Daddy's leather belt. He never had to use it on me and Isaac, but boy if we didn't take off running when he looped it over his hand and told us to start acting right. That was almost never.

Isaac and I were good boys. Mama told us that all the time. Even when I broke her favorite snow globe cuz Isaac and I wanted to taste the purple juice inside it, she was sad and mad, but she said I was a good boy. I was a good boy because I felt so sad about hurting something she loved. I did a bad thing, but I felt real sick about it. Bad boys would feel happy when they did mean things, my mama always told me. God forgives you if you say I'm sorry and mean it.

I was trying to be so quiet, sitting there on the closet floor, hoping maybe these people would just forget about me and leave me here. I didn't want to go live with Aunt Millie. I tried to explain I could make my own food, and school was only a few blocks away, and I knew how to take a shower by myself, but these people weren't listening to me. They told me little boys need a family to look after them.

I already had a family. I didn't want a new one. Isaac and I could look after ourselves. Nobody was ever going to replace Mama and Daddy. I already had the best family in the world, even if it was only for seven years. It was time for me to grow up now.

"I don't like being in here, Pete," my Aunt Dot said. "I feel like I'm being watched. I can feel 'em here."

Maybe that's why I liked being in this closet so much. I could feel 'em here, too. Ever since the accident, this was my spot. Maybe if I wished hard enough they'd come back long enough to tell me what I was supposed to be doing with my life.

*"Be tough but kind," my dad would tell me. "Don't let anybody take advantage of you, and you don't ever take advantage of somebody weaker than you are just because you can."*

*"Be nice to animals and old people," Mama would say. "And make sure you always have on clean underwear in case you get in an accident."* This was just me making stuff up. Being silly. Being a weak boy.

"You watch too much TV, Millie," Pete said. "They're in the dirt. They're not gonna come back and haunt you for getting rid of Bobby Jo's old ratty jeans."

Uncle Pete was right. Last week, they dropped us off to

school on their way to work at the factory, and now they were in the dirt. If I'd known it'd be the last time I'd see 'em, maybe I woulda told Mom to take a picture. She liked to do that, but we men always whined. I didn't even remember what she was wearing that last time I saw her. If it was those jeans Pete was talking about, I needed to know. Maybe it would help me remember.

Feeling bold, I kicked open the closet door.

"Judas, baby," Aunt Millie said, reaching out her arms to hug me, "what are you doing in there, mister? Why aren't you helping Isaac get your toys packed up?" I ducked to avoid her kisses. She was going to pretend to be my mom now, but I didn't want my mom to think I was okay with it, especially if she really was here in this room.

"Don't throw her clothes away," I pleaded, grabbing the jeans from her hands. "Don't throw her away." She had tears in her eyes, and it made me feel sad, too.

"We're not throwing anything away," she said, sitting down on the edge of the bed. "We're going to put it all in boxes, though. We're gonna put it in a safe place, and you and I can go visit whenever we want. Does that sound alright?"

I shook my head. I wasn't trying to be bad, but I didn't want to visit my mom in a shed. I didn't want to go visit the hole my parents were in. I wanted everything back to normal.

"Mommy! Mommy!" my cousin Burt shouted. My heart stopped beating when I saw what he was tossing up in the air and catching in his hand. I felt red, like I was turning red, like I was seeing red, and I couldn't move. "Look what I found!"

Isaac and I collected cans all summer to buy my mama a new snow globe just like the one I broke. It had a pretty fairy inside that looked like her and was full of purple and pink glitter juice, ugly girly stuff, but she loved it. She loved this one even more than the first one because her good boys gave it to her.

"Burty, be gentle with that," Millie said. It was too late. It smashed off the hardwood floor, glitter juice flying everywhere. I wanted to hit him. I wanted to choke him. I hated him. I ran back into the closet and slammed the door behind me, burying my face in the fabric of the Christmas dress.

## 2

## Judas

"Come on, Jude, it's your turn!" Isaac said, handing me the Game Boy. He must've known I was very sad. He never wanted to share with me before. It didn't make me feel any better, though. I didn't want to play a dumb game. Stuff like that didn't matter anymore. I turned and looked out the car window. Everything was farm and trees. "Jude, come on. Why don't you want to play?"

"I want to go home," I said.

"That's not our home anymore, brother," he whispered. Aunt Millie was up front driving, and he looked in the rearview mirror, making sure she wasn't listening to us over her Christian rock music. I didn't like how excited he was to move to the farm. No matter how many times he explained to me about how rich Aunt Millie and Uncle Pete were, or that we'd get our own rooms, or that our cousins always had the newest video games, I didn't want any of it. He was a traitor to Mom and Dad. He thought he was upgrading his life. He was so stupid.

We didn't have a mom and dad anymore, but Aunt Millie and Uncle Pete were going to be our new mom and dad. They already had kids, though. Isaac didn't understand we were outsiders. We'd never have a mom and dad again. I stared at the trees harder, thinking maybe if things turned out like I expected I could always go live in the woods by myself.

When we got to the farm, it looked like a carnival in the driveway. There was a bouncy house and a clown, and loud music playing from a speaker. There were people everywhere. Kids I knew from school, old white-headed ladies I knew from church. It looked like a big party.

"What is all this shit?" I stammered. I slapped my hand over my mouth. I never said that word out loud before, and it felt really bad.

"It's your welcome home party, boys," Aunt Millie said. She didn't mention my swear. She was trying hard to be nice as possible to us. She was throwing us a party with all the things she thought we would like. My parents would've never been able to afford to give us a party like this. We always had our birthday at the bowling alley or the YMCA.

The laughing kids, the loud music, the goofy clown who was bending balloons all around, I hated it all. It made me angry. She wasn't just trying to make us feel welcome, she was trying to show us she was better than our parents. Our dead parents.

She wasn't though. Not her, not Uncle Pete. I hated this stupid house. It was too big. I hated this stupid circus. I took my stupid blue balloon and threw it on the ground and started stomping on it until it popped. I screamed, I cried, I waved my arms. "Shit!" I yelled over and over again, as if saying it once gave me the entitlement to say it whenever I felt like it. The more I yelled, the better it felt.

Everyone was staring at me. Nobody said a word, just looked at me with sad eyes like I was an animal in a cage, too stupid to be responsible for my actions. I knew why they were looking at me like that, but it didn't make it any better.

"Knock it off, Jude!" Isaac said, looking like he was about to cry himself. "You're ruining everything." I knew at this very instant in my seven-year-old mind that he was not my brother anymore. He was one of them. I was all alone in the world. He wasn't just 'making best of the situation' like the therapist lady told us. He was all in. The twin brother I grew up with was as dead to me as my parents were.

I took off running, running as hard as my little legs could carry me. I'd always been fast, but I got tired really fast. My lungs burned and I choked back my tears. I ran until I found a little hutch. I knew this was the chicken coop from the times we'd visited Aunt Millie's farm. There were birds everywhere, pecking and squawking all around. I opened up the door, and there was a big fat gold hen inside sitting on a nest.

She looked at me and cocked her head to the side, blinking her beady little chicken eyes right at me. I don't know why, but I felt towards that chicken what I thought my mom and dad had felt toward me. She didn't look like she was scared of me, she wasn't angry at me like my brother was, or confused by me like everyone else in the world had become. The way she squawked just a little bit and bobbed her beak at me, I knew she liked me. I knew I loved her.

"Hey, little chickie," I said. I didn't know how to talk to chickens. I didn't know the first thing about 'em except that I liked 'em covered in barbecue sauce. "What are you doing, girl?" Only a little ray of light shined through the crack in the coop, but I saw what she was doing clear as day. She stood up and underneath her was an egg.

"Wow," I said, whispering to her softly. "Is that your baby?"

She blinked at me, knowingly, and sat back down on her nest. I curled up in the straw, and even though I was just a kid, it wasn't really a comfortable fit for me in the little coop, my head nearly hitting the wood ceiling as I rested by back up against the wall. It smelled pretty bad in here, and it wasn't really comfortable, but I felt like this was where I wanted to be. This was where I belonged. She clucked contentedly, and I just shrugged, closing my eyes and falling asleep next to my new friend.

## 3

## Judas

"She's not laying eggs anymore, boy," my uncle Pete said. "You think we keep these things for our health? How do you think we put food on the table, son?"

I wasn't doing too good adjusting to living on the farm. I didn't like having my own bedroom. It just reminded me more and more how alone I was in the world. Isaac was having the time of his life, acting like my cousins were his true kin, and I spent most of my time that summer hanging out with the animals, watching and feeding the chickens, making sure their eggs got picked up before the other animals could get into them, helping Aunt Millie brush the horses, and chasing the goats around. I heard what the kids said about me, calling me chicken boy, calling Goldie my girlfriend and making kissing noises at me whenever they saw me.

I just told them to fuck off. I liked the way it sounded.

I was ready for school to start in the fall. At least I could be near my friends again.

All the adults around me were treating me weird, too. I had to go to therapy all the time. Nobody told me no anymore. Everyone acted like they were partly scared of me and partly sad about me, and I was learning to use that power to get what I wanted. That's what happens when both your parents get murdered in a shooting at the factory.

Uncle Pete wasn't budging, though.

"You can't kill her," I said. "Look at that pretty face." I picked up Goldie in my arms. She didn't like it, kicking her claws all around and pecking at me. "This is for your own good, pretty. Be nice."

"Put her down, Judas," he said, his tone irate. "She don't like that. Now you got her all riled up. Put her in the pen with the others."

"Is it time yet, Paw Paw?" my cousin Burt shouted from across the field, his face bright red from running. Isaac was right behind him, along with Cindy and Sarah, the older girls who tortured me the most out of all of 'em.

"Almost, son," Uncle Pete said, grabbing Goldie from my arms in one swift tug, squeezing her around the neck.

"Stop it!" I screamed. I wanted to punch him, but I knew that was a fight I'd never win. Uncle Pete was the size of an oak tree, and I'd seen him put the whooping on Burt before. The only thing I could hope was that Goldie could outsmart him. I knew she had it in her. He wasn't exactly the brightest man. "Flap your wings, Goldie! You can do it!" There was no use to my pleas. He took her and tossed her over his shoulder into the pen with the rest of the chickens he was going to slaughter.

"Come on, Paw," Cindy teased, "let him have one last date with his girlfriend." The kids started to laugh and point at me. Isaac and Burt got in the pen with the now-panicking chickens, who were gibbering and squawking and flapping wildly.

"Just like I showed you guys," Uncle Pete said. I

watched through my fingers as the boys picked two birds up by their claws and flipped 'em upside down. Uncle Pete took his knife, making slits on the sides of their throats as more blood than I'd ever seen in my whole life started shooting out everywhere.

"Sick!" Isaac shouted, tossing the dying bird to the ground as it flopped all around in its blood.

Sick is what I was. I didn't even realize I was throwing up down the front of my shirt until Sarah pointed it out. "What's wrong, little precious boy? You forget where chicken nuggets come from?"

I knew I wasn't supposed to put my hands on girls, so instead I started running to the house.

"Aw, come on, Judas!" Isaac taunted behind me. I looked over my shoulder and he had Goldie by the feet, whipping her around in the air like a yo-yo on a string. The sound was the second most horrible thing I'd heard in my life up until that point. Just a little bit less bad than the sound of the police officer explaining that my parents were never coming home from the factory. I knew one thing was for certain. I was never eating meat ever again.

## 4

## Judas

We had to wake up at 4:00 a.m. to get all our chores done and get on the school bus on time. Even though Aunt Millie had spent the last two weeks making us get up extra early for practice, I couldn't keep my eyes open on the ride to school.

We were the first group of kids picked up, and for the next hour, the bus bumped through the back roads, tossing my breakfast around inside my stomach. I closed my eyes and imagined what life would be like if Mom and Dad were still around. I'd still be in my warm bed, Isaac sleeping on the top bunk. Dad would come in and flick the lights on and off and make silly foghorn sounds while we grumbled. He'd help us get cleaned and dressed and Mom would have my favorite waffles ready when we finally came downstairs.

Here at the farm, we had to take care of ourselves in the morning. Ourselves and the animals. All the poor animals who didn't know they were just here to keep my cousins fat. I made it my goal to at least give them the best life possible while they were here. That, and to never eat them, even though everyone teased me constantly and even called me ungrateful.

Just one more thing that drove Isaac and I further apart. Every time my aunt made chicken for dinner, he'd ask if it was Goldie or just one of her kids while he stared at me and laughed. I didn't break in front of him anymore, just stared at him as hard as I could, wishing my eyes were filled with laser beams and I could blow his head off with my thoughts alone.

At least at school I could be around my friends again. They didn't call me 'chicken lover.' They had no way of knowing what happened over the summer. We could play stick hockey and ride bikes just like we did back in the good old days. Back before the shooting.

As I snoozed away on the bus, hugging my backpack to my chest, I awoke to the worst smell I'd ever smelled in my life. I blinked my eyes open, the bus nearly filled to the brim with kids all around, some I knew, and some who were much older than me.

"Wake up, chicken kisser!" my cousin Burt shouted as he smashed the hard-boiled egg into my mouth before I even saw it coming. "Hey everybody! This guy wants to marry a chicken!"

I choked on the nasty taste in my mouth, spitting the egg out in his face. Roars of laughter filled the bus, and everyone started making chicken sounds. Isaac was the worst. I'd never forget the way he was pointing and laughing at me, screaming 'chicken kisser!' I grabbed Burt by the collar of his shirt and clenched my fist, holding it inches from his face.

"I'll fucking show you," I said, my voice deeper than I'd ever heard it before. "Your mommy and daddy aren't here to protect you."

"Yeah, well your mommy and daddy are dead," he

said defiantly. The bus grew silent as he said that. I didn't know what was worse, being known as chicken kisser, or being known as the boy with the dead parents, but neither one was how I wanted to start off the school year. I was done being anything but the kid that nobody messed with.

I swung back and smashed my fist into his face, hard enough that I heard his tooth crack.

Everything starting moving in slow motion. The bus stopped. Isaac grabbed me and tossed me to the floor. The driver was dragging me up the aisle. Burt was screaming, blood running down his face, clenching his front tooth in his hand.

The driver tossed me in a seat up front. I knew I really had it coming when I got to school, but I didn't care. This was how it was going to be from now on.

I didn't know the kid in the seat next to me. He looked like he cut his own hair, buzzed on the sides with a long rat tail that hung down his back. He smelled like my dad used to when Mom would pick him up at the bar after third shift, like dirty old cigarettes. He pulled his headphones off his ears and sneered at me.

"You really fuck chickens?" he asked. I had never heard anything so gross in my life, but it rolled off his tongue so naturally, like this was the kind of stuff people talked about at his dinner table.

I ignored him, stared ahead at the bus seat in front of me, pretending like I couldn't hear him.

"I asked you a question, boy. You a chicken fucker?"

"Leave me alone," I said.

"Or what? You gonna knock my teeth out, too?" He smiled wider, showing me his missing two front teeth. "Did that myself. Well, with a string and a door. Needed me some tooth fairy cash so I could go to the movies."

## Judas

"You're crazy," I stammered, partially in horror, partially in fascination. This was a tough guy.

"You fuck chickens," he said with a shrug, laughing at my obvious irritation.

"I don't," I said. "Quit sayin' that."

"I don't care if you do or don't. You gotta good punch. We're gonna be good friends. My name is Quentin," he said, holding out his hand. He looked to be about my age, but I never seen this kid before. I shook his hand.

"I'm Judas."

"If you're gonna be a tough guy, Judas, you gotta learn how to control yourself. You want to punch that asshole, that's cool, but don't do it on a school bus. There's cameras here. You can always talk yourself outta anything as long as there's no evidence." I looked at him wide-eyed. Maybe I had taken things too far. I probably needed to go apologize to Burt. I wasn't tough enough to be a part of Quentin's gang. "Why do you think I had to come to this shit hole school? I flashed my knife around at recess and the wrong person saw and the principal found it in my backpack later. Never leave evidence laying around."

"Understood," I said, looking all around, trying to gauge how far we were from the school. This guy was way out of my league. I didn't want to be the kid nobody messed with if it meant ripping out my own teeth and carrying a knife around.

"I didn't like that school much anyway," Judas said. "The bitches were much cuter there though. You got some real heifers around here, huh?" I didn't know what he was talking about.

"I'm eight, dude," I said. "I don't look at girls like that."

"So just chickens?" he taunted. "Girl chickens, though, right?" I went back to ignoring him again, holding my backpack tight to my chest, tapping my foot on the ground, knowing my fate at the end of this ride wasn't a good one. "I'll stop," he said. "I'm gonna teach you so much stuff, Judas. We're gonna be best friends."

"Okay," I said, hoping it would shut him up.

"You don't gotta worry about anything if you hang out with me. Nobody's gonna pick on you. If you're my friend, I got your back for life. It's in my blood. We're brothers now."

I didn't understand what he was saying, but I agreed with him, even though it felt like I was making a deal with the devil. I was going to need as much help as I could get, a scrawny guy like me who had dead parents and didn't eat meat. My home life was probably going to get a lot worse once Uncle Pete heard what I did to Burt, too. "Fine," I said. "We're brothers now."

The school bus slammed to a stop, and I got up and stood in the aisle. "You coming?" I asked him.

"You go ahead," he said. "Everything's gonna be okay. You understand?" I stood outside the bus, watching the kids get off, shoving past me, pretending like they couldn't see me. I planned on just turning myself in once I got into the school, no need for the bus driver to make a scene. Burt stepped off the bus, his hand planted firmly over his mouth, and I reached out to him.

"I'm sorry," I said. He just shook his head and kept walking.

Quentin followed shortly behind him and winked at me as he wandered off. The bus driver closed the door and drove off. I was so confused. I didn't know if I should go to the principal's office myself, or pretend like nothing had happened, just like everyone else was.

I had no idea what this Quentin character did, but he

was good on his word. Now I'd have to make good on mine.

I spent the day waiting to get called to the principal's office, nearly jumping out of my chair every time the teacher called on me. Nothing happened. Nobody said nothing to me. I hid out in my room most of the night, knowing that certainly Uncle Pete was gonna take his belt out and give me a good beatdown for ruining Burt's face. Still, nothing. Nobody at home said a word, not even his sisters. Rumor had it he was telling everyone he fell. So were Sarah and Cindy.

My brother, Isaac, was the only one who had anything to say, when he snuck into my room late that night, pinching my nose shut and covering my mouth so I woke up gasping for air.

Even then, "You're ruining everything, asshole," was all he said before sliding out the door, closing it softly behind him.

# 5

## Judas

"You gonna come pump iron with me at the clubhouse?" Quentin asked. It's what we usually did on Thursdays. Now that we were twelve, we needed to start working on our muscles for the bitches. Quentin's dad had a gym set up in the garage of the house where his motorcycle gang lived, and he let us use it a few times a week so we could work on our lifting.

"Gotta go straight home today," I said. "Aunt Millie's doing the pictures for the family Christmas card."

"Sounds fucking lame," he said. He pulled a cigarette out of his pocket and brought it to his lips. I looked all around nervously. We were standing in front of the school in broad daylight. He didn't care, though. He never cared. Part of me loved it, and part of me was just afraid of what would happen if I ever dared to cross him.

Turned out running with Quentin was pretty okay. I never had to fight; nobody at school dared pick on us. Maybe we came off as creepy. Bitches didn't seem to mind. I was a bad boy by proxy, and even at twelve, the old mantra rang true. Bitches loved bad boys.

## Judas

At school, I was popular. At home, I was the odd man out. My cousins and brother had written me off a long time ago. They didn't mess with me in public. They knew better. At home, they pretty much ignored me. I kind of liked it.

"You wanna come with?" I offered. One thing I knew about Quentin was that he got pretty lonely if we didn't hang out after school. He didn't like being left alone like me.

"Nah. Sarah and Cindy are real woofers," he said. "If I wanna see floppy titties I'll just hang around the clubhouse. Maybe see some nice ones by accident, too."

He was pretty obsessed with titties. I guess I was, too. He was right; my cousins weren't anything special. Nothing like the ladies who ran around the clubhouse. "Suit yourself," I said. "Will you ask your mom if I can stay at your place this weekend?" It was pretty normal anymore. Usually, it was just the two of us at his parents' house while they did club stuff so we just 'babysat each other'. Sometimes his kid sister, Athena, hung around, but she was a weirdo and still played with baby dolls. As long as nobody needed stitches at the end of the day, we could pretty much do whatever we wanted.

Aunt Millie didn't know quite what to do with me anymore, so she didn't seem to mind shipping me off. It was easier this way. I was just biding my time till I was old enough to get a job and move out. Never see any of those jokers again.

"You know you're always allowed. You're my brother," he said. It was something he said a lot. That's what all the men in his dad's club called each other. It felt more real when he said it than when I talked about my actual brother. We were brothers because we wanted to be. Loyal till the day we died.

I probably would've hugged him, even though it was the pussy thing to do, if I had any idea what was going to happen in the next twenty-four hours.

# 6

## Judas

Family photos were stupid, but Aunt Millie took them extra serious. Her annual Christmas card was her pride and joy, and this year she dressed us all up in these nerdy white turtlenecks with girly little red felt vests. We looked ridiculous. She looked so happy though, so I played along. I didn't have nothing against Aunt Millie. She was just doing the best she could every day, but now that all us kids were getting older and more expensive, and Uncle Pete got laid off from his job, they didn't have the cash flow they used to and it was stressing her out. I could tell by the way she wasn't eating much anymore, making sure all us had enough on our plates.

Nobody was ribbing me about not eating meat anymore, mostly cuz the rations were getting slimmer for everybody as a whole. Quentin did talk me into drinking milk and eating eggs sometimes, only because he read in a muscle magazine that protein made your muscles bigger. I figured I was doing the cows a favor anyway when I milked them. Quentin also told me bitches loved having their titties squeezed. I made sure I talked real sweet to them while I did it. Practiced my game for when the time came I'd get to milk a real girl.

We took our family pictures. We ate an awkward dinner. Uncle Pete started with the beer, the girls busied themselves with their sewing, and I went up to my room and got to work on my math assignment before I had to do my evening chores.

I took up most of the animal feeding and shit shoveling, but I didn't much mind. I liked being around the horses and pigs and cows and chickens much more than I liked being around the woofers that were my girl cousins and the pussies that were my brother and Burt.

I thought about changing out of my stupid family photo outfit before going out to the barns, but figured if I ruined this shit, I'd never have to wear it again. I knew exactly what Quentin would say if he caught me in this outfit. My teacher said we weren't supposed to call people homos because it's hurtful, and I wasn't trying to hurt anyone's feelings ever, but I didn't see any straight men running around in red felt vests with tassels.

I laced up my shit-kickers, shouted into the kitchen that I was going to go do my rounds, and walked out the back door. It was getting late, the sun starting to set in the September sky, turning everything a weird shade of purple. "What ya doing up there, Mom?" I asked, thinking maybe her and Daddy were trying to get my attention. I liked to think they were having an alright time, hanging out with Jesus and my grandparents I never met. I liked to think they watched over me, but only when I was being good, and never in a creepy way. My mom and dad didn't need to know what I did in the shower.

I was snapped out of my moment of talking to the clouds by the strangest sound I'd ever heard in my life. I could tell it was one of the mother hogs by the loud pitched squeals and grunts, but this wasn't her normal chatter. She was in distress. My heart sank, thinking maybe something bad happened to one of her babies. Maybe it got kicked or stepped on by one of the bigger animals. Her cries were chilling, and I sprinted down to the barn as fast as I possibly could, hoping it wasn't too late.

I could hear my brother and Burt's laughter from outside the door. It was even more chilling than the sow's wails. It was a cruel kind of laugh, the kind only a maniac would have. I threw the barn door open, and it took everything in me not to throw up when I saw the scene unfolding in front of me.

Sally the sow was chained up to the metal fence, a piece of chain around her neck like a noose pulling tighter and tighter as she thrashed and fought, gnashing her teeth and digging her hooves into the dirt floor, choking herself as she tried to break free, pure hatred in her eyes. My brother had one of her baby piglets, barely the size of a house cat, by the leg, as Burt took the branding rod my father used on the cows and seared it into the flesh of the tiny pig's stomach. It was kicking so hard, its leg had to be broken, the smell of burning flesh searing my nostrils.

"What the fuck are you doing?" I shouted, running towards my brother, grabbing for his wrist. The poor piglet was squealing like a crying baby, and mama sow hadn't calmed down at all. Its flesh was marked all over in those brands, like this torture had been going on for quite some time.

Burt pointed the bright red-tipped rod at me. "What's wrong, chicken kisser? You like pigs now, too?"

I kicked him in the shin and he wobbled backwards. "You guys are being cruel. This is what you do for fun? Torture baby animals?"

"Aw, come on, Judas," Isaac said. "They're just dumb pigs. They don't matter."

I punched him in the stomach over and over. He let go of the piglet and fell to the ground, crying so hard he puked. I would've punched him some more, my heart filled with rage, but I needed to take care of Burt first. Take care of Burt and get Sally free before she strangled herself.

"Knock it off, Judas," Burt said, snickering as he flicked at the blow torch and held the tip of the branding rod over it. "Don't think I won't use this on you if you even try to come near me."

"You're a fucking pussy, Burt," I said. "You know better than to fuck with me." It was true. Him and my brother were scrawny and weak. They weren't real men. They had to pick on little animals because they knew they'd get their asses beat if they tried that shit on anybody else. I scooped up the little piglet off the floor of the barn, and carried it over to Sally, who immediately began to weep like I'd never heard an animal weep before. I patted her on the head, rubbed my hand through her dirty fur, whispered to her that everything was going to be okay, doing my best to sooth the anxious mother while her baby suffered at her feet. "Put the damn rod down. You proved your point."

He lunged past me and jammed it right in between Sally's eyes, as she reeled backwards in pain, snorting and howling. He was laughing that maniacal laugh. Everything around me turned red, and I made a promise to myself that it'd be the last time he ever laughed again.

I caught him off guard as I knocked the rod out of his hand and it hit the floor with a loud clank. He stood there, paralyzed with fear. I picked it up off the ground and he put his hands in the air, walking backwards towards the barn door.

"Come on, Judas," he said, his voice much higher than

## Judas

it was a few minutes ago. "We were just screwing around. My dad brands the animals all the time. You know that."

"Your dad brands 'em because he has to. That ain't what you were doing here, you bitch." I inched towards him slowly, holding the rod out in front of me. He reached for the door, but I was faster, slamming it shut with my boot and walking him towards the wall. "I oughta kill you, Burt. I oughta take this rod and chop you up into a million pieces and feed you to Sally."

He cowered in fear, dropping to the ground in resignation, his hands covering his face.

I should've just let it drop.

Why couldn't I just let it drop?

He learned his lesson. He knew better than to do this shit ever again, I was certain by the way he'd just pissed his pants. I couldn't let it drop, though. The rage flowed through me as I drove the rod into the flesh of his stomach, pushing hard as it sizzled against his skin and he screamed like a little girl.

I couldn't let it drop as I took the rod and began beating him repeatedly as he rolled over onto his stomach and tried to crawl away from me. "You wanna know what it feels like to be afraid for your life, Burt?" I shouted. "You want me to get your momma in here so she can watch you get tortured?"

I was crying by now, every lash of the rod, every kick with my boot breaking me more and more. I lost all control, of that I was certain, and I didn't know if I hated him or myself more right now. I was so lost in my rage, so gone, I hadn't realized my brother had ran for help.

I didn't even notice my Uncle Pete tackling me to the ground, pulling me off Burt. My aunt wrapping his twitching body in a blanket, screaming for the girls to go get the car. My brother crying in the corner. So much chaos. I sat down in the straw next to Sally and petted her body, watching the chaos unfold around me, in complete shock of the nightmare I'd just created.

I sat in the barn with Sally and the dying baby piglet until the red and blue lights flashed in the driveway. When the cops came and handcuffed me, the only thing going through my mind was that I wished I wasn't wearing this vest as they toted me off to the station.

That was my final day on the farm. That was the last time I ever saw Sally. All my years in juvenile detention I liked to think maybe she broke free that night, took her babies with her. I couldn't bring myself to think she ended up on Burt's breakfast plate.

# 7

## Judas

"You have a visitor," the officer said, standing in the doorway of my dorm. I'd been on good behavior, the best behavior, the whole time I was here. I was never a bad kid, but someone charged with 'attempted homicide', no matter the fact they were only twelve, no matter the fact that the asshole was out of the hospital by the end of the weekend, had to be treated with a certain amount of cautiousness. I got it. I always did what I was told. Always played their little games. Kept my nose buried in books and stayed away from the thugs and wannabe gangsters. I didn't know what the next year was going to bring, only that I was sixteen and fixing to get out of this place any time now. What came next was completely out of my control, just like what time I was allowed to go to the bathroom or what I was going to get to eat.

"Who is it?" I asked. Nobody really came to visit me here. Only visitors I was allowed were family, and it was pretty clear they were done with me after the incident. Even my own brother only visited once in all four years, and he barely said three words in the whole twenty minutes, staring at me like I was some kind of monster.

Twelve-year-old me thought he was the monster. He was the one that testified against me in court, told the judge and jury how I was yelling "I oughta kill you" when I attacked Burt. I could've been off on a misdemeanor charge if it weren't for him. He was the fucking Judas in this situation.

Sixteen-year-old me, I've had plenty of time to sit with this shit. Plenty of time to realize he was just protecting what he knew. He had a roof over his head, the love of his family, everything a boy could ask for. I was the one who was going to ruin it all for him. I was the problem. So, he got rid of me. I made peace with it long ago.

I was surprised to see him in the visitor's room, waiting there for me nervously. He looked worse than I did. Skinny as hell. Still weak. His clothes were dirty and his hair was long. I reached out to hug him and he flinched.

"What are you doing here?" I asked. "Haven't heard from you in a long time."

"I'm sorry," he said. "You know they don't like it when I... well... you know."

I knew exactly what he meant. Obviously Aunt Millie and Uncle Pete weren't my biggest fans. "It's alright, Isaac."

"I feel guilty," he said softly. "I did this to you."

"That's just something you're going to have to live with," I said nonchalantly, immediately regretting my choice of words. It sounded bitter. It sounded like I was holding a grudge. I wasn't. "It's fine. I swear. Juvenile detention hasn't been so bad to me, to be honest. Wish there were some better-looking bitches around here, but I'll survive. Besides, I'm getting out soon."

"That's why I'm here," he said, pulling out a couple of

folded-up sheets of paper from the pocket of his jeans. "Aunt Millie wanted me to give these to you." I unfolded it and shrugged, looking over the petition for emancipation. "She said she'd pay for whatever court-wise."

I had long assumed I wasn't going to be greeted with open arms when I got out. The paperwork solidified that, forcing me to face the fact that soon, I was going to have to start a whole new life, on my own.

"She doesn't want ya to have to go into the system," he said. I laughed. It was funny. I was already in the system, and she didn't seem to worry much about it for the last few years. Maybe she's just trying to make herself feel right about the choices she'd already made for me. I'd give her that. It was the least I could do for jacking up her son. Maybe it was the opposite. Maybe she wanted to send a sign that, no matter what happened, I wasn't to be coming around the family anymore. I was on my own in this world.

"Thanks," I said. We had this weird little stare off for a while, and even though the years had changed us both physically, even though I was big and jacked out of lack of anything better to do in here, and he was weak and tiny, our eyes said the same thing. He looked lost. I was lost. I often wondered what life would've been like for the two of us if Momma and Daddy never died in that shooting. Would we still be here, like this?

The guard entered the room, twirling his finger, urging us to wrap it up. I nodded to Isaac and made my way to the door.

"Where are you gonna go?" he called after me. I just shrugged and let the officer put my cuffs back on. "Is there something I can do?"

"Be good," I said. "Don't get yourself mixed up in this shit."

He hung his head, and I pretended like I didn't notice

him crying as I walked out of the room. I don't know why the fuck he would cry over me. He got everything he wanted. In a way, I did, too. I never wanted to live on that farm, never wanted to pretend Millie and Pete were my parents, I'd rather go through this life alone than have to live a lie. The paperwork tucked into the pocket of my jumpsuit would guarantee me that. My golden ticket to complete aloneness.

# 8

## Judas

The guards were sad to see me go.

So were my cellmates.

If I was good at anything so far in this life, it was being in jail. Looking back on my time served, I was kind of impressed at everything I'd accomplished. I got my GED. I lost my virginity to some sweet little blonde bitch on my fifteenth birthday while the guards pretended like they heard nothing, best three minutes of my life so far. I worked out hard, doing push-ups, pull-ups, and squatting and bench-pressing anything that wasn't bolted to the floor, my muscles bigger than I'd ever imagined them being. I learned to cook. Learned to barter. Learned to get by with nothing but my personality and smarts.

I had a feeling the real world wasn't going to be so easy. My free ride was over. I was sixteen, a convicted felon, and emancipated. I had nowhere to be and nothing to do but figure shit out.

I never expected Quentin'd be waiting outside juvenile detention for me the day I got freed. He was sitting there in this neon green hooptie, a cloud of pot smoke rolling out the slightly cracked window, Slipknot blasting so loud the side mirrors looked like they were about to rattle off the frame.

The passenger door flung open and Athena, his little sister, hopped out, rolled her eyes at me, and got in the back seat. I stood there with my hands in my pockets and a grocery bag of my belongings, consisting only of one felt red vest and a white turtleneck, slung over my arm.

"You gonna get in?" he asked, his smile looking like something a comic book villain wore. Of course I was going to get in. I had no other option, right? This was the only choice in front of me right this second, the only future for me. I had no idea what kinda hell he was going to be dragging me to, but as of today, Quentin Fisher was my only friend in the world. I'd go wherever he took me.

I hopped in the car, pulled the door shut, rested my head back on the seat, and sighed.

"I missed ya, buddy," he said. "The fuck did they feed you in there? You look like a tank."

"He looks like a man's supposed to look," Athena said, cracking her bright pink bubblegum up against her cherry red lips. She'd definitely grown up in the last four years. She looked like a woman was supposed to look. I didn't have much going for me, though, and trying to get in my best friend's sister's pants probably wasn't going to help my situation. "Now drive, asshole. I told Dylan I'd be at his house an hour ago."

He gunned the motor of the weird old car. It's nothing I'd ever expect to see him in, between the orange shag carpet and the fuzzy dice hanging on the rearview, but I guess times had changed. "Where'd you get this thing?" I asked.

"Old Q-Tip won it in a bet. He wouldn't be caught

dead in it, but the bitches seem to like it alright," he said, shrugging.

"The bitches do not like it alright," Athena said. "At least, the kind of bitches who don't walk around with chlamydia. I feel like I need to hose myself down with bleach whenever I get out of this piece of shit."

"You need to hose yourself down with bleach before you get into this, sis. I don't want the kind of crabs you carry around getting in a fight with the native species."

"You're fucking gross," she said with a snort.

"Well I'm fucking hungry now," Quentin chuckled. "What do you want for your first meal as a free man?"

"Not seafood." I made a fake vomit sound and we all cracked up. "And not because I'm a vegetarian."

"Still on that, eh?" he asked, raising his eyebrows. I was on it for life. How could I not be? I'd sacrificed my childhood for my beliefs, as twisted as it was. If I quit now, I'd have damn near killed my cousin for no reason. That wasn't me. I was always a man of principles. "What the fuck do you eat then? You want me to take you out to a field so you can chew on some grass?"

"How about you take me somewhere I can get some fries and a milkshake? Somewhere that has real ketchup, not the generic shit."

"Generic ketchup," he said, shaking his head. "You poor thing."

He stopped in front of a tattered old trailer and Athena hopped out of the car. I couldn't help but admire her long tanned legs and her round ass, just barely covered by her worn-out cutoff jean shorts, as she walked away and disappeared inside.

"I want details, brother," he said, turning down the volume on the radio. "Did you drop the soap?"

I laughed. "A boy never kisses and tells."

His face turned white as a ghost and he clenched the steering wheel.

"I'm fucking with you, brother," I said. "Nobody wants to fuck with a guy who almost murdered his kid cousin. Except all the crazy broads from the girl's center." I shot him a wink and he relaxed. "What the fuck have you been up to?"

"Working. I got kicked outta school and now my old man says I gotta earn my keep. Gonna take over the family business someday. Gonna be the boss of the club someday, too. I got it all planned out. Now that I got my business partner back, shit can start happening."

At the moment, I had no aspirations for my life, and it sounded like a good enough plan for me. He had a job lined up for me and everything. Maybe someday I'd figure out what I wanted to be when I grew up, but for now, easy sounded good. Business partner. Brother. Only person who showed up the day I got outta jail. He promised me he'd always have my back, and now, he was making good on that promise.

I didn't realize I'd spend the rest of my days making good on my part of the deal.

# 9

## Judas: Age 20

We were celebrating Rudy, our enforcer's, sixtieth birthday in the best way we knew how. Colt's old man, Q-Tip, president of the Indignant Few MC, rented out the good tit joint, the one that was a little bit out of the way, tucked up in the woods, an 'anything goes' kinda place where all the bitches had all their teeth. The owner had no problem accommodating groups of guys like us who had the kinda cash to keep their lights on and put their dancers in brand-new cars. Bitches here were always happy to see us. They were extra happy today because it was only the twenty or so of us.

Colt, Q-Tip, and myself were in the VIP room, walled off from the rest of the place. I didn't give much thought to my best friend and his dad's boners right next to me in the darkened room. Shit like this was normal. It was who we were. Ain't no shame in the pussy game so long as it weren't attached to anybody else's property.

"I gotta get back to the house, boys," Old Man Q-Tip said. The topless brunette writhed in his lap, her desperation for his undivided attention almost endearing. Quentin's father, his attention was always divided all over the place. One eye on the club, one eye on the road, his heart with Quentin's mom, his dick in a club slut's mouth, both his hands firmly steering the family business. I definitely admired the old fucker, the closest thing to a dad I'd had since I was a kid. I definitely wanted no part of following in his footsteps. That was Quentin's job anyway.

Quentin was called Colt now. Myself, they called me Judas still. The old times thought it was funny somebody could be so cruel as to name their kid after one of the most hated men in history.

We were the newest patched members of the Indignant Few MC. It seemed like a logical progression for me. Colt had taken me in as a brother before I even knew what it meant. Now, I had a real family. A family I was willing to do anything for.

"Your momma's having problems with Athena," he said to Colt, reading the texts as they popped up on his phone. "Honey, get down," he said to the stripper, who hopped off his lap with a whiny grunt and stood there with her arms crossed, pouting. "You're a sweet girl, Bella." He kissed her hand and she smiled at him. Q-Tip was the kind of man who really knew how to smooth things over with the bitches. Every woman I knew loved him—the girls at the strip club, the lady that did the taxes for the business, random women we came across walking down the street, they'd drop whatever they were doing and make excuses to talk to him. Every damn time.

It's not that he was that good-looking. Years of hard manual labor, years of drugs, sex, and violence, years of sleeping with one eye open, it all showed in the creases on his face, the gray of his beard, the wrinkles and sun spots on his forehead, but for some reason, he had this thing, this unstoppable charisma that made him the best possible president for our club, this aura that made people just want to do whatever it took to be a part of his world.

He put us young bucks to shame, landing the kind of pussy we only dreamed of, and at the end of the day, he went home to Reena, the queen of the club, toughest woman I ever met and drop-dead gorgeous, not just 'for her age.' If it weren't for the fact that Q-Tip and Colt would both toss my ass in a woodchipper, I wouldn't think twice about doing things with that woman.

Instead, I got this blonde twit who was bouncing on my lap so hard, I was lucky she didn't get me hard because she probably would've snapped my dick in half about two songs ago. She had those big old fake titties that kind of had a mind of their own, always moving about three seconds behind the rest of her body as she gyrated, defying the laws of physics. Yeah, I was timing it in my head. Staring not so much in admiration, but fascination. I definitely wasn't feeling like this was the kind of bitch I wanted to take back to the clubhouse with me.

"You need a hand?" I asked Q-Tip.

"Do I need a hand with my seventeen-year-old daughter?" He laughed and stroked his beard, shaking his head at me. "I've seen where your hands have been, son. If you want to keep 'em, you better keep 'em far far away from my Athena."

Colt chuckled. "Old man, if only you knew," he said. Q-Tip shot him a daring look and he turned his attention back to the two women in black g-strings.

"You think she's okay?" I asked, once his father left the room. Athena was a smart girl, but she had a mind of her own, to a fault. More stubborn than Colt, she was going to do what she wanted to do, when and how she wanted to do it, even if it wasn't in her best interest. She was quick to throw the fact that Q-Tip and Reena weren't necessarily the most hands-on parents in their face. "You let me raise myself as a child," she'd say, point-blank, emotionless, "don't pull that mommy and daddy shit on me now." And, "Blade got emancipated when he was sixteen. Are you trying to say he's more mature than I am? Or is it because he's a boy?"

Always pushing the power dynamics of the club. I knew she didn't like the way her old man ran around on her mom; she'd confided that much in me. I knew she hated the whole 'club slut' thing, because a constant point of contention was the fact that it was okay for us to screw around with whoever we wanted, it was just what men did, but everyone was quick to judge her actions.

Even under the guise of 'she's just a teenage girl,' anyone could read between the lines.

She was just doing what her old man and her brother did, and was constantly getting punished for it. It was an unfair world for Athena, and every day I felt her slipping further and further away, looking for any reason to escape the life she'd been born into. I didn't want her to go, but I'd never beg her to stay. I tried to find a happy medium, tried to help her apply for colleges nearby, and helped her with her homework whenever I could. Probably it was selfish. Probably I just wanted to keep her around because I liked her. I liked being around her, at least. She had the looks of her momma and the charisma of her dad, and Colt's sense of humor. She wasn't like these fake-titted bitches who wanted us bikers for what we were.

She was the kind of person who was satisfied with who I was. Not the patch I wore, or the bike I rode. Me, as a person, not as a collective. Selfish me, and there was nothing I was ever going to do about it.

"She'll be fine," Colt said, peeking his head out from

behind the dirty duo sandwiching his body. "Now shut up. I'm not trying to think about my sister right now. Family shit don't belong in the strip club."

It *was* a man's world we were living in. You could grope tits next to your dad, and nobody'd think anything of it. Athena wasn't a person, she was a woman. No matter how much we loved her, she was just the same as these broads we used for our pleasure, except she was off-limits to all of us. I understood perfectly fine why she was sad all the time.

Out of nowhere, screams began to echo through the entire building, loud enough to permeate the thick steel door separating us from the main room. Screams of a hundred strippers, it seemed.

"Old Rudy probably took his pants off," Colt said with a chuckle. The music stopped suddenly. I jumped up from my seat, pushing blondie aside. The lights overhead went from dimmed to full blast, and a fire alarm began to wail. The hair was standing up on the back of my arms. My heart raced. This was definitely not Rudy flashing his dick to some unsuspecting girl. Shit was going down.

The four girls in our room now started panicking, screaming, crying, looking to us for answers. "Is the place burning down?" one asked. I put my hand up to the door. It felt normal. I breathed in, trying to catch a whiff of smoke, but all I could smell was cheap perfume and arousal, the usual fragrance of places like this.

"It's gonna be alright, ladies," Colt said, grabbing his pistol from the table before tossing me mine. I pulled the door open just a little bit, peeking through the crack before quickly slamming it shut again.

"Fuck," I stammered. "Motherfucker."

As much as Q-Tip was revered by the ladies and by his Indignant brothers, there were at least as many men out there who hated him. Hated him to the point of wanting to see his ass in a hole. Or in this case, tied to a stripper pole with a gun pointed to his head. No matter what happed in the next minute, people were going to get hurt. People were going to die.

The only thing that mattered right now was minimizing the carnage that these men in black masks with machine guns could inflict on all of us trapped in here. My brothers. These innocent women.

"What?" Colt asked, his eyes the size of saucers. He stood behind the door with his pistol out as I pulled it open once again for him to look. "What the fuck?" he

"Girls, get in that closet," I said. "Don't come out til me or Colt comes and gets ya. Don't come out for nobody but us." They were a mess: bawling, makeup running everywhere, naked limbs flailing all around. Why weren't Colt and me acting the same way? This shit was heavy.

"What's going on?" the redhead wailed. "Are we going to die?"

"Get in the fucking closet and try to be quiet," Colt growled, holding the door open and gesturing inside, "or you're probably gonna die." I shot him a look of death. No sense in getting these bitches more worked up than they already were.

"Not cool, dude," I whispered, as he shut the door behind them, barely muffling their sobs.

"What's not cool is that our fucking club just got caught with their dicks out, literally. What do we do now?" I was at a loss myself. None of our officers were nearby to tell us what to do. All we had to go on were the Indignant bylaws that had been beaten into our heads over the last two years. We needed to protect our brothers at all costs, but we needed to protect these innocent bystanders first. Club rules. No civilians get dragged into our shit ever if we wanted to keep our legacy going.

## Judas

The sound of machine gun fire ripped through the building and my body grew tense, blood pumping through my veins as I double-checked that my pistol was loaded and the safety was off. "We do what we're supposed to do, Colt. We handle shit."

## 10

## Athena: Present Day

I slammed the keyboard with my fist, mashing the keys of my laptop and swearing under my breath.

*Fucking idiot, what the hell were you thinking?*

My desperation had got the best of me. My paranoia was at an all-time high. *Harold had to know exactly what I was doing, right?*

For whatever reason, he seemed oblivious to my mission, even though I kept pushing things a little bit further every day. If he was, in fact, watching me closely, my most recent internet search history was definitely going to be the last nail in my coffin. I didn't know what possessed me when I searched 'how to fake your own death,' but the second I did, I had a feeling I wasn't going to have to fake anything.

"Babe, what are you doing in here?" Harold asked, walking into my bedroom. I tried to hide my disgust as I looked over at the poorly aging man with the cheesy mustache and gray chest hair pouring up over the collar of his polo shirt, his thick gold chains getting lost in the tangled mess.

## Judas

When I met Harold ten years ago, seventeen-year-old me thought he was the slickest and sexiest man on the planet. He rescued me from following in my momma's footsteps, saved me from that shithole small town, and whisked me off to Vegas. I often wondered if Harold himself really was that sexy, or if it was just the idea of him that I was so infatuated with back then, because now, to me, he was just a creepy old pervert. Just like the rest of 'em. Just like the men I left back at home.

I think, these days, he looked at me the same way.

I was, after all, no longer a naive seventeen-year-old. Making myself attractive enough for the industry was a full-time job between the gym, the hair, the tan, the makeup, botox, plastic surgery, whatever it took. In his eyes, I was getting increasingly more high maintenance every day. I wasn't sure if he was just getting too old to get a boner naturally, or if he really just found me that repulsive now, but a night of wild fucking these days took at least a few Viagra for him and a copious amount of blow and a bottle of scotch for me.

Still, he was tender towards me. Maybe it was because he was a sentimental guy. Maybe it was because I was the only person who knew how to run our business.

I wasn't an idiot. It was all by design.

"Babe!" he said again, grabbing my wrist softly, moving it from the laptop. He lifted my fingers to his eyes. "You need to fix your nails."

"I'm working on it," I said, jerking my hand away. One fucking chip in my black nail polish and you'd think I was ruining his life. "I'm trying to get last-minute promo pushed out for tonight. Shiloh Splinter is in town last-minute and she wants to go live with the girls."

"For real?" he said, his jaw nearly hitting the floor.

"You're a miracle worker. She's a legend. Hell, you could probably sit tonight out if you wanted to."

I raised my eyebrows at him. Of all the rude things he'd said to me over the years, that was the one thing that pushed my buttons the worst. "It's my show, Harold," I said, as if he needed reminding.

My weekly webcam show was the whole reason why our 'promo' company was as big as it was today. We got in early, before the big online porn boom, before you could find anything you wanted for free with the click of a button. Back when we were living in a hotel on the strip, back when there weren't webcams or camera phones and we had to film with a digital camera and plug it into the laptop to upload it like barbarians. My savvy nature helped us keep up with the changing times, and my legendary status and familiar face kept our early customers from straying. I was a mainstay in hundreds of thousands of horny dudes' and ladies' bedrooms every week for the last ten years. I might not perform as much anymore, but I at least had to make an appearance.

"That it is," he said, smiling faintly, his gold incisor catching the light off my computer monitor. God, he was fucking shady.

Then again, so was I. I had to be, though. I was the reason why this business was what it was today. I worked my ass off and showed my ass off to the entire world to get us where we were. He could try and tell me I was easily replaced, that there were much hotter and younger chicks out there who could easily do my job, but in my heart, in my soul, I knew it was always all about me. Sure, these people liked pussy, but they also liked me as a person. Why did he think we were constantly booking big-name porn stars on the show? Why did he think everyone who'd had

## Judas

an appearance on the show went on to do great things with their careers?

It certainly wasn't because some sketchy-looking dude with a mustache and a gold chain promised them a life of riches on his dirty director's couch.

*It's always been you,* I reminded myself, reaffirming the rationale behind my recent indiscretions. One more big show, one more big cash grab, that's all I needed to blow this joint and move on with my life. I'd been skimming from some of our shadier clients for a long time now after I figured out a pretty slick way of hacking our database. It was never much, a few bucks here and there spread across a whole bunch of prepaid cash cards, but all that added up. I was finally getting paid what I deserved, enough to get me out from under this scumbag and buy myself a quiet chunk of land somewhere in Montana, where I could meet a nice cowboy and live happily ever after, nobody to answer to but my horses and goats.

There was a pounding on the front door of the apartment, loud enough to startle both of us. "Who the fuck knocks like that?" I asked.

"It's probably just one of the boys being stupid," he said. "I sent Billy out for lunch a little bit ago."

"Did you have him get me something?" I asked.

"You have yogurt in the fridge. And salad. Why the hell do I spend all this money on tummy tucks for you if you're just going to eat yourself into a coma?" He shook his head at me condescendingly, like I was a total moron. I wasn't going to miss that look.

I wasn't going to miss the yogurt. Or the salad. Or the supplements that made me shake or the laxatives that made me feel like I was going to shit my pants 24/7. As soon as I hit the state line, I was stopping for a cheeseburger the size of my head.

Harold could kiss my ass. I'd feel bad for my fans for a little bit, but they'd get over it. I'd introduced them to plenty of new chicks to wank off to. Maybe someday, once everything blew over, I'd make a comeback. On my own terms.

"You gonna answer that?" I asked, the pounding on the door getting louder by the second. "They sound like they're getting impatient."

"Finish up whatever you're doing and start getting ready," he said. "I'll call Leslie and tell her to squeeze you in for a manicure. And an upper lip wax." He pulled the door shut behind him.

"Fuck you!" I screamed after him, hoping he heard me.

*Fuck you with a rusty hammer.*

*Fuck you with a stick of dynamite.*

*Fuck you with a garden hose full of gasoline.*

I was amusing myself with the mental images I was conjuring, but I didn't have time for that. I had all my valuables tucked into my backpack. I had prepaid bank cards and wads of cash, enough money to live out my days like a queen. I slid my laptop into the bag, zipped it up, and stuffed it under the bed, ready for my great escape tonight.

*Where the fuck is that barking coming from? We don't have a dog.*

It sounded like some massive beast was wrecking my living room, barking and snarling, and Harold was screaming like a little girl. I cracked the door open, not daring to step outside. Four men dressed in black hoodies and full blown ski masks, men I'd never seen before in my life, were towering over Harold as he laid on the floor, his hands over his face.

I tried to scan their faces through the tiny crack I left in the door, but nobody looked even remotely familiar. The way they were dressed, they could've been anyone's goons.

Anyone with any kind of money had a squad of men who weren't afraid to fuck somebody up.

Which reminded me, *where in the hell were ours?*

*Probably stopped for dessert, because they didn't have to worry about their figures like I did. Those fuckers.*

"Where is she?" the tallest of the men shouted as he crouched down over Harold, spit flying from his lips. "Where the hell is she?"

"In the bedroom. Second door to the left," he said, without hesitation.

*I hope they kill him anyway, just for fun,* I thought. I slammed the door behind me, and grabbed my already packed bags. *Well this is fucking convenient.* It'd always been my natural talent knowing when it was time to call it quits, time to leave, knowing when I'd overstayed my welcome and it was time to move on with my life. I didn't mind burning bridges to the ground on my way down. This blessing, this foresight, this God-given talent, might have saved my life a couple times in the past. It was definitely going to save my life today.

I had no idea who these goons were. I had no idea who they worked for or what they wanted from me. Surely nobody would be coming around trying to shake me down over a missing hundred bucks or so. I knew how much a crew like that cost by the hour. It wasn't cost-efficient. This wasn't some petty theft shit. This was something more serious.

What it could possibly be? I wasn't sure. All I knew was that my ass needed to shimmy out the window right now. I left my cell phone laying on the bed and grabbed a sundress from my closet. I'd change as soon as I knew I lost them. A porn star running through the streets in her bathrobe, even in Vegas, was enough to catch somebody's attention.

I crept across the yard, slinking down in the bushes of the backyard, trying to get a good feel on the place. If my daddy taught me anything before he died, it was always know your surroundings at all times. If he would've practiced what he preached, he might still be around today. I wasn't blinded by cash or pussy like him though. I had my life savings strapped to my back and there was nobody in this world I wouldn't throw under the bus right now to protect my own ass, whether they had a pussy or a dick. It was go time.

I crept through the hedges, crawling around the edge of the fenced-in yard, staying low to the ground. My bathrobe was probably flopping wide open, and I kept getting poked in the eye by twigs. I damn near shit myself when a little bird flew out of the shrubbery right in front of my face. Could've been a bullet. I already had my nose reconstructed once before; I didn't feel like playing that game again.

Then again, depending on who these guys were, that might be my only option, going full-blown incognito. Shit, I didn't know what was plastic and what was real on me anymore anyway. Maybe I could find someone to strip me down to my studs, let me go back to being boring old Athena, the kind of chick who wears sweatpants to the grocery store and always has chipped fingernail polish from tearing apart motorcycle engines.

*Definitely no more motorcycle engines*, I reminded myself. Never again. I'd lived that life long enough. Burned that bridge to the ground.

A loud ringtone emanated from my backpack. "Shit," I stammered, completely forgetting the burner I carried with me. I ducked down low in the bushes. Speak of the damn devil.

"Mama," I whispered, "I can't talk right now. I'll call you back in a little."

"What are you doing? Are you running? Since when do you run? You weren't answering your regular phone; that's why I called this one." Reena never understood the concept of 'I'm busy.' My dear mom just assumed it was an excuse to get off the phone with her. Sometimes it was. I looked back and forth before leaping through the shrubs, into the neighbor's backyard, sprinting as I cradled the phone in my neck.

"Mama, shit is going down," I said. "Somebody's after me."

"What did you do?" she asked. I could tell she was puffing away on a cigarette. Probably sitting on the porch swing looking for some gossip as usual. Last I heard, my brother was doing a glorious job of fucking up his life. Why couldn't she harass him.

"Why you always assume it's my fault?" I ducked behind the chaise lounge near the pool, using it as a shield as I tried to see if anyone was following behind me.

"Is it your fault?" she asked.

"Probably!" I said. "I gotta go. I gotta grab a cab. I gotta get out of the city."

"You can always come home, you know. You still have a bedroom here. I miss having you around."

I sighed and shook my head. She really did still think there was a chance I'd move back home after all these years. Truth was, I'd rather turn myself over to the men who were back there looking for me than ever move back to the clubhouse with what was left of the gang.

"When I get where I'm going, Mom, I promise, you can come live with me. I'll buy us a big old house in the middle of nowhere, and we can have chickens and horses and whatever you want. You and me, a fresh start."

"I can't leave here, baby. You know that. The club needs me."

In the past, we'd fought til I was blue in the face over the fact that the club did not need her. At all. My dad was long dead. All the club life did was take from her. Her freedom. Her sanity. Her dignity. Now that Q-Tip wasn't around, they didn't need her anymore. She needed them. She didn't know what else to do, and she was too brainwashed to listen to her daughter.

"I gotta go, Mom. I'll call you back when I get on the road."

"Be careful," she said. "I love you. You're going to be alright. You always are. My strong girl." So calm. So collected. Only a bitch who'd seen some shit would be that put together in a situation like this.

Just like I was.

"I'll see you soon, lovebug," she said, and hung up the phone.

*Wishful thinking, Mom.* Nothing in the world was going to make me go back to that life ever again. I'd rather die alone than spend my days and nights constantly worrying about club business, caring deeply about people and watching them die. I've seen all kinds of hurt in my day, but loving somebody just to see them ripped away by the choices they make, that's the worst kind of hurt.

"Dammit!" I screamed as the wasp nest fell to the ground in front of me, an angry swarm of stingers buzzing around my head. I must not have noticed it hanging off the side of the pool house, and as I shuffled to dig my sundress from my backpack, I must've jarred it loose.

*Always be aware of your surroundings, you fucking moron.*

"Dammit!" I shouted again, the first stinger digging into my arm like an angry jolt of electricity. I slapped at it instinctively as another one zapped me in the ankle. I took off like a maniac, sprinting through the yard, my bathrobe flying open as I stumbled over my feet. I couldn't catch a break today. I'd never been stung before. For all I knew, I was deathly allergic. I'd always had a sneaking suspicious this would be the way I'd go out, tits flapping in the air, running away from something or someone. Today it was both.

I was manic by the time I hit the front yard, the only thought in my mind waving down the first car I saw and having them take me to the emergency room as a precautionary measure. Knowing my condition, nobody would pick me up, and if they did, straight to the nuthouse for me.

That ceramic lawn gnome popped up out of nowhere.

*We don't even have lawns here,* I thought as I was going down. *Who the fuck has a random gnome laying around?*

My foot caught on it, and I was eating concrete before I could even put my wrist out. This was surely it. Between the wasps and the bad men, my lack of shoes, and my probably broken ankle, I was toast. Even if I did make it out of here alive, surely creepy Harold would find me, and I wasn't sure I'd be able to talk my way out of the backpack full of cash and credit cards I was carrying. I closed my eyes and tried not to laugh through the tears, the ridiculousness of it all, every inch of my body throbbing in pain.

I sprawled out on the concrete, trying to figure out my next move, when I felt something wet on my toes.

"What the fuck kind of sick pervert is licking me right now?" I groaned. The way this day was going, nothing would've surprised me at this point. Nothing, except the face that was smiling down at me like a jackass as I picked my head up.

"How have you managed to keep yourself alive all this time, sis? You're a fucking mess."

"Colt?" I asked. I had to be hallucinating. I hadn't seen my older brother in damn near seven years. I was hoping to go at least another seventy. I wanted to lay back down and play dead, but the damn dog that had been licking my toes was now slobbering in my ear and it was really uncomfortable. There was no dignified way of doing this. I tried to tug my robe tight so I wouldn't flash my brother in the process of sitting up.

"Are you surprised?" he asked.

"You're a fucking dick," I said.

"That's no way to talk about your brother, Athena," he said, offering his hand to me. I slapped it out of the way and tried to push myself up from the ground, but the struggle was more than I could handle. "Besides, it was Mom's idea."

"Well she's a fucking cunt," I quipped. He curled his lip like he was grossly offended before nodding in agreement and falling into a fit of laughter. "She really put you up to this?"

"She was worried about you. She said you haven't been acting like yourself on your web show lately," he said.

"Gross. She watches my show?" I tried not to throw up in my mouth. I really really should've changed my name before I got in the business.

"I'm just fucking with you," he said. "At least, I hope. Reena misses you, Athena. She wants you home. She said the only way you'd probably come is if we kidnapped you."

"You came all the way out to Vegas to kidnap me?" I asked. It seemed so silly. I knew my mom could be a lot to handle, but I knew Colt had about as much interest in seeing me as I did seeing him.

"Nah, we came out to Vegas for business. Figured we'd make a pit stop on our way home. Now get your ass up off the ground. Your little pimp should be waking up any minute now, and I'm sure he'll be looking for you. Probably gonna be curious about the sack of cash and the burner phone, I'm assuming."

God, he was observant. At least my daddy didn't die for nothing.

"I was getting out of here anyway," I confessed. "I'm not getting on your bike, though. That's just weird. And I'm not going home, either. Y'all can dump me in Nebraska and I'll figure it out from there."

"That's not how this is going to work," he said, reaching his hand down for me once again. "I'm not your ride service. You come home and see your mom and make her happy, then you can do whatever you want to do."

He pulled me up from the ground, and I cringed as I tried to put weight on my ankle. We hobbled through the front yard and I used him to support my weight, as much as I didn't want to. Maybe it wouldn't be so bad. Maybe a couple days at home to figure out my next move would be good for me. I did miss my mom. I did miss my girlfriends. I definitely missed the Amish bakery.

"Thena, why is your face swelling up like that?" he asked. I slapped my hand over my cheek. My right eye was swelling shut and starting to leak down my face.

"Wasps," I said. "I'm allergic to wasps I guess." To my horror, I was staring down a group of guys I didn't recognize out of my good eye. I'm sure a few of them were the men who broke into my house. They were all dressed in the Indignant leathers, and all looked to be about my age. It was a weird feeling.

Growing up in the club, all the men were my dad's friends, a bunch of old beer-bellied bikers with yellowed beards and missing teeth. Now my brother had taken my father's position. Now, those men were his friends. Those men, well, if I was just thinking with my lady parts and not my brain, I wouldn't mind taking a ride on the current iteration of the Indignant Few train.

I knew better, though. Soon enough, these men would all turn into my father. I'd met better adjusted porn stars than I had bikers. This life was not a kind one. Soon enough, these men would be cheating on their wives, pissing off drug cartels, and neglecting their kids. I lived it. I knew it firsthand. History repeats itself.

Nobody was in a hurry to say anything to me, but I was used to that by now. It happened every time I went out in public. I knew most of them had probably seen me naked before, doing dirty things they probably enjoyed but would never admit, especially not in front of my brother.

"Does your eyeball always look like that?" a tall guy with black hair who looked like he had a tendency to say stupid shit asked. "I mean, you must have a really good make-up artist, is all. Very cool."

Another man, 'Law' written on his patch, obviously the enforcer of the club by his stature alone, punched him in the stomach. "You're having an allergic reaction," he said, with the type of confidence that led me to believe he was a very smart man. "I told you idiots this was a bad idea. Do you know what you got into?"

"Wasps," I said.

"How is your breathing? Does your throat feel tight?" he asked. He reached for my neck to feel my pulse, and I pulled my bathrobe tight, suddenly aware of the fact that I was standing on the sidewalk in broad daylight straight-up flashing a bunch of strangers. It probably would've made for an epic episode of my show, if my show was still a thing.

"My throat feels fine," I said. "I can breathe just fine." He swung open the door to the big red truck that was pulling the trailer and pulled out a first-aid kit. "What are you, a boy scout or something?"

He fished out a couple pink tabs and a couple white ones and handed them to me. "I was a medic," he said. "This should make you feel better. I got an EpiPen in here if you start to go into anaphylactic shock. We'll just have to keep an eye on you for a little bit."

He handed me a water bottle and I put it to my lips, taking down the pills.

*I wouldn't mind playing doctor with him.*

Of course I never would. None of these guys.

"We gotta hurry," Colt said, nodding to the men to get on their bikes. "Long ride ahead."

I'd forgotten how much I hated that rumble. That low, loud, roar that had the street vibrating all around me. I was starting to feel a little woozy, and realized I was using this 'Law' guy's hard body to keep me upright. Now he was helping me into the truck, the truck pulling the trailer full of Lord knows what, and I didn't have it in me to argue or fight.

Sleep was the only thing I could imagine doing right now.

Maybe this was all a bad dream and I'd wake up and life would be back to normal. I'd go back to my porn show, and back to plotting my escape. Maybe my brother and his men freed me from that life, but knowing I was stuck on the road with them for as long as it took to get across the country felt worse than being in jail.

"If she starts having trouble breathing or if her lips start swelling up any more, you pull over immediately," Law said to the guy in the passenger seat. I opened my good eye and looked all around. The face staring back at me in the rearview mirror gave me chills. I had never forgotten that face, those serious deep blue eyes that held all the world's sorrows and yet never once complained. I guess in my fantasies he escaped the club shortly after the incident. In my fantasies, he had a wife, kids, a farm, a boring nine-to-five job, he was far far away from everything that ever hurt him.

Why was he driving the truck? That was a task usually assigned to prospects. Times must have changed significantly since my dad passed.

"Judas?" I spoke softly to the set of eyeballs in the mirror. I was ashamed by the way I looked right now. I never thought I'd see his face again. I hoped I'd never see his face again. I was sure, out of everyone I knew, my life choices probably disappointed him the most, and it made my heart hurt.

He didn't look too good, his face thin and pale, his hairline creeping back up his skull. He looked like he'd aged thirty years in the seven since I'd seen him. He'd never looked at me the way he was looking at me now, with amusement, like I was pathetic and helpless. He'd never made me feel that way before, even though everyone else in my life was quick to.

"No, doll." The man spoke in a voice that was like a watered-down version of the rich deep voice of the real Judas. "I'm Isaac. We went to high school together. Remember me?"

My skin crawled. The memory of Judas's twin brother was one I had buried deep inside. He'd always been kind of a creep. Him and his cousin thought they were God's gift to women, and whenever my girlfriends and I saw them coming, we scattered because we didn't enjoy their groping and taunting. Besides, he was a nark. He was the reason why Judas had to go away for all those years. I guess people could change, but the way he was licking his lips and snarling made me believe otherwise.

"I'm retired now. Moved back home to be closer to the family, and Judas got me into the club."

"First of all, you didn't 'retire.' You got fired from an amusement park for whipping out your dick and peeing on a bush while you were in your costume," the guy in the passenger seat said. This guy looked so young, baby-faced almost, the kind of good-looking that screamed surfer more than badass biker. His hair was dark brown and shoulder-length, and his smile was friendly in the warm kind of way. God, had times changed. "Second of all, you're still prospecting. Maybe if you get the cargo back in one piece, we'll meet about it. I'm Breaker, by the way."

"The cargo," I groaned. "What are we hauling today? Heroine? Machine guns? Sex slaves you smuggled across the Mexican border?" If we got pulled over, I'd tell the cops in a heartbeat that they kidnapped me, too. I wouldn't think twice about it.

"Sorry, toots," Isaac said, pulling out a toothpick and resting it on his lip. "That's not something for bitches to know."

The other kid punched him in the shoulder and he winced. "Don't listen to him. It's nothing to worry about. Just a bunch of industrial cleaning equipment."

"Which is code for?" I asked.

"Literally. Big janitorial company got shut down a few months ago, we came out here for the auction of their equipment. Got some industrial-grade shit for the business."

I couldn't believe what I was hearing. Mom had told me Colt had been working hard at turning dad's demo business into something more lucrative, but I assumed by that she meant illegal.

"Yeah, so we can clean up murder scenes easier," Isaac quipped.

"What the fuck, dude?" Breaker muttered. The way he shook his head made me think he wasn't lying. I had given my brother a little too much credit. Isaac began to go off on a tirade of the inner workings of the club, talking about how not only did they demo houses, but they got rid of people that needed getting rid of, explaining in great detail the scientific method of how to dispose of dead bodies. Real CSI shit. Fortunately, this medicine was making me woozy enough that I didn't catch much of it. I pretended like I was asleep as he jabbered away. As soon as we got off the road I needed to warn Colt. There was no way a guy like this one, a guy who was obviously trying to show off for me, was worthy of the patch.

What the fuck did I care, though? This wasn't my circus. I didn't even want to be here. These idiots had the audacity to break into my home and stage a kidnapping that I didn't even ask for. These idiots were the reason why my eyeballs were swollen shut.

These idiots were the reason why I was going back to the one place I swore I'd never go back to, and yet for some reason, I wasn't even putting up a fight.

I could blame it on the drugs, but that wouldn't hardly be the one hundred percent truth. No, there was one other reason that might bring me home. That reason looked kind of like the man who was driving me there. Sounded kind of like him, too. If I closed my eyes and blacked out the words coming out of his mouth, I could pretend for a second, like I'd done so many times in the past.

## 11

## Judas

I grabbed the blacklight and did another once-over of the abandoned warehouse while Miles packed up the equipment and tossed it in the dump truck.

"You about done, brother?" he asked. "I'm fucking beat." It had been a long day. Our friends, the brothers of the Dead Ringers MC, were having a rat problem, and they needed to call in an outside exterminator. Eight hours of interrogation, and all we had left was a couple garbage bags full of bloody body parts. That, and a huge favor coming our way. In this life, favors were worth more than cash, and alliances were more precious than anything money could buy. What better way to show our stance on loyalty to the patch than to rip apart a couple traitors limb by limb.

I picked up a clump of hair from the concrete floor with a little chunk of scalp still attached. I choked back the vomit in my throat. It wasn't so much the act of murder that got me, but the aftermath made me fucking queasy. Bits and pieces of body parts were gross to me. Reminded me of the deli section at the grocery store, everything all hacked apart and randomly wrapped up again. I dry heaved as I slipped the traitor's head skin into the plastic baggie.

"You alright over there?"

The building smelled chemical, and the only fingerprints left behind were the ones that were there long before we got here, likely from the local gang of 'witches and warlocks' who came out here to try and summon demons. I hated to break it to them, but hell wasn't some magical place where they would finally meet their master, Satan. Hell was here on earth if you were willing to look hard enough. Demons walked among us. We dealt with them every day.

We took the random pile of scrap metal in the bed of the truck, using it to cover up the garbage bags. Nobody ever stopped and searched us, but the last thing we needed was a stray head to fly out the back and smash into somebody's windshield. We didn't need that kind of publicity. The Indignant Few weren't the loud and flashy type of bikers. We laid low, kept our heads down, and did our work. Our business was as much legit as it was dirty work, and we blended just fine into the neighborhood. No drama. No blowback. From the outside, we were just a bunch of guys who demoed buildings and rode motorcycles. From the inside... things were a little different.

"You heard from the crew yet?" I asked. A bunch of the guys went out to Vegas for an auction. Miles, Delaney, and I hung back to take care of the business and keep an eye on the clubhouse. It was fine by me. I didn't have much interest in going to Vegas. Betty Sue, my ex, just got out of rehab, and as much as I didn't want to be with her anymore, I felt like it was my duty to keep an eye on her and make sure she stayed clean.

"Nah, it's still early out there, though," he said, wiping

the rust from his hands onto his jeans. He hopped into the driver's side, and I slid into the passenger seat, reaching for the joint in my pocket. "What do you wanna do now? Probably the house is gonna be quiet tonight. Wanna go down to Marble's? See some titties?"

I sparked up the joint and shot him a thin smile before putting it to my lips. "Not in the mood for titties tonight," I said. All I wanted was a hot shower and a cold beer at the same time. "Besides, we still got some work to do."

"Eh, I figured Delaney could handle it," he said. "Pretty boy never gets his hands dirty. He's probably back at the clubhouse putting his dick in something that ain't his old lady, pretending like he's holding down the fort."

"That, or passed out on the couch," I said.

"Dreaming about cheating on his old lady."

"What the fuck do you care?" I asked. "You got beef or something? Since when are you the morality police?" I didn't much care for the way a lot of the guys in the club treated their women, but at the end of the day, it was none of my business. "You jealous?"

He looked frustrated, like he was about to say something he was going to regret. I passed him the joint and he took a big hit, filling the cab with smoke. We rode the rest of the way home in silence. Sometimes it was better to just put a stop to things before they turned into bigger things. We were so good at destroying evidence in our day jobs, we knew better than to make messes at home. Less was more, especially when it came down to bitches.

I hopped out to unlock the gate, and we pulled down the long gravel driveway that led to the clubhouse. He parked the truck in the garage, closing the door behind us as we sat in darkness and silence for a minute, trying to snap out of the day's events in case of who might be inside. You never knew who might be hanging around, and they didn't need to know where we were or what we were doing.

"Called it," I said, spotting Delaney passed out on the dingy sofa, his hand tucked in his pants as he snored louder than a chainsaw. I tried not to chuckle at the three women playing cards at the table, all in various states of undress. Colt's mom, Colt's wife, and Colt's girlfriend were in the middle of a heated game of strip poker, not even acknowledging the two of us. I was personally thankful. I wasn't in the mood for anybody tonight.

I fished a beer out of the cooler for myself, cracking the top and sucking it down. I slipped another one in the pocket of my hoodie and headed off to my bedroom.

"You boys hungry?" Reena called over, looking up from her handful of cards. I tried to pretend like I couldn't see her nipple slipping out of her black lace bra. I swear her face was the only thing on her that aged over the years. She was still Colt's hot mom, no matter how old she got. "I'll go heat ya something up."

"I'm good," I said. "I'm going to my room. Holler if you need me." I slapped Delaney on the thigh and he jumped upright, looking all around like somebody just fired a gun. "Got a surprise for ya in the truck."

He groaned and zipped up his pants. "No worries, chief," he said, throwing me a salute.

"Night, everybody," I said, walking down the long dark hallway to my bedroom. I put the key in the stainless steel door and instantly relaxed. Cold, dark, super clean, just how I liked it. I knew the time would come that I'd need to move out of this place and get a house of my own, but for now, clubhouse life suited me just fine. This had been my room since the day I got out of jail. I wasn't really a sentimental man, more a creature of habit. I liked living here just fine. Plus, I felt a lot better being able to keep an eye on the club 24/7, up close and personal like a vice-president should.

I slid out of my clothes, cussing at myself for wearing one of my favorite t-shirts. I knew Reena could get blood outta anything, but I'd rather just burn it. That stain would always be there in my mind. I didn't like dirty, stained things. I tossed it in a ziplock baggie and slipped it in the freezer for safekeeping.

I flexed in the mirror as I waited for the water to warm up in the shower. Ever since Betty Sue went to rehab, I'd been hitting it pretty hard in the gym, and it was showing. I'd always been a muscular guy, despite everyone telling me I needed to eat more protein to get any real gains, but now I was a fucking tank.

*Great, dude, you have a nice body, but who cares?*

The club sluts liked the way I looked. Most women did. I could get my dick wet whenever I wanted, but it didn't matter. I'd only had one real girlfriend in my life, and I fucked her up so bad with my inherent sadness, my sickness, she'd overdosed more than once. Over and over again, I brought her back to life so she could suffer with me. Breaking up with her was the kindest thing I could've done, even though I still paid her bills and looked after her a year later.

I opened up my second beer and stood in the shower, letting the water run down my body, washing off the day's indiscretions. I still hadn't heard from Colt. They were supposed to get back sometime tomorrow. It was lonely around here without the rest of the crew. I didn't do too good with people leaving, even to this day. So many people coming and going from my life as a kid fucked me up good. The shooting at the strip club reinforced that. Everybody bailed on me eventually, or I cut 'em out before they had a chance to get too close so I wouldn't have to lose 'em. Not Colt, though. Not the new Indignant Few.

I finished my beer in the shower, a little drunk from not eating, a little more than tired from a hard day's work.

*Oh shit,* I thought, drying myself off. *It's Thursday.* I brushed my teeth quickly and slipped into a fresh pair of boxer briefs.

Thursday night was the night that Athena's webcam show was always on. I knew some of the other guys watched it, purely for jerk off reasons, but it wasn't something we'd bring up in front of her big brother. She had a hot body, and the stuff she'd do on camera was kinkier than anything I could even wrap my brain around. She was the best at what she did.

I didn't watch it cuz it turned me on, even though it did. I watched it cuz it was all I had left of her. I didn't realize until after she ran out on the club how much she meant to me. Maybe it was because her, Colt, and I spent so much time together driving around, getting high, goofing around, talking about our dreams. Something about her brought me back to a place in time where my life could be whatever I wanted it to be. I still had no idea what that was, but every time I tried to imagine it, she was there.

It was silly, hanging on to my childhood crush into my thirties. Hell, she was never even really my childhood crush. She was just the girl in the jean skirt who always wanted dropped off at some random guy's house. My best friend's sister. But to me, she was home.

I flipped open my laptop and brought up the website. I paid for a membership a long time ago using a throwaway card, a throwaway name; she didn't need to know I watched her. She'd probably think I was a creep. Not that I'd ever see her again.

Lately, there'd been something off about her. I hoped

## Judas

maybe she was just going through a phase. I honestly had no idea who she lived with, if she was married, what she did in her spare time. I liked to imagine she was on her own, surrounded by people who loved her as much as she deserved to be loved as she built her porn empire. She'd always been tough as nails. She deserved all the success in the world. Lately, though, she'd seemed distant. Sad. Maybe I was reading into things. Maybe Betty Sue getting clean was doing something to my mind, making me want to find another stray to fix.

Something wasn't right with the website tonight. This episode that was showing was an old one, one before she got the most recent tit job. This had never happened before. I clicked around thinking maybe my computer was malfunctioning. I could've sworn she was promoting tonight's show all day on social media. Maybe I was losing it, because I checked her Twitter and everything was erased.

My phone rang and I jumped out of my chair. It was Colt. He couldn't have known what I was up to. He was a crazy fucker, but I highly doubted he'd had my computer hacked. Unless he liked watching me beat my dick every night before I went to sleep, I didn't think he'd put a camera in my room.

"What's up, brother?" I asked, slamming the monitor shut. "Where you guys at? Everything okay?"

"We stopped for the night in Kentucky," he said. "Should be back before noon tomorrow. Everything's good. Got ourselves a smoking deal, nobody got shot, and I'm pretty sure I'm not bringing home any new STDs."

"Well that's great," I mumbled. "I'm sure your wife and girlfriend will be so proud. You know they're hanging out together tonight?"

"Fuck me," he said. "I'm a dead man." I just laughed. I

knew things were complicated with his wife, Zelda. She was brought up in a motorcycle club as well, and she had a tendency to be really fucking crazy. Tressica was the ray of sunshine in his darkness, the woman who got his soft side, the woman who I knew, deep down, he loved more than even his mama. While she was well aware of Zelda, I wasn't sure if that was reciprocal, or if Zelda just assumed she was another club slut. Beat the shit out of me. It was way too much drama for my liking.

"They seemed to be getting on alright," I said. "Everything else was alright too."

"Cool," he replied. There was no need to get into details on the phone. "Thanks for taking care of shit, man. You always got my back."

"Sure do," I said.

"I got a surprise for you," he said. "Something you'll really love."

"You left my brother somewhere in Nebraska?" I asked.

"Yeah right, you know that fucker would find his way back somehow."

He was right. I figured Isaac would've broken down awhile ago. When I agreed to let him prospect, it was me trying to be the bigger man, trying to let go of my past, but he was turning into a huge pain in my dick. The only thing he had going for him was his willingness to do whatever we told him to do, and when you're in a business as dirty as ours, it was good to have guys like that around.

"Is it gonna get me put back in jail?" I asked. I could only imagine with him. For all I knew, the trailer was loaded up with illegal immigrants or exotic reptiles or who knows what the fuck else he could come up with left to his own devices.

"Probably. Jail or the ditch. I can't wait to see how it turns out."

"Great." I muttered. "I'm going to sleep. Hit me up if there's anything I can do."

"Make sure Zelda and Tressica don't kill each other?" he asked.

"Anything other than that," I said, hanging up the phone. That was definitely not my circus.

I wanted to ask him about Athena, if he had heard anything from her or about her, but I knew he'd probably just bust my balls. Every time I'd said something to him or Reena recently, they just shut me down. Something was off tonight, though. She'd never missed a show in the past except when she was recovering from plastic surgery. Even then, she had guest co-stars. It was probably nothing. It was definitely none of my business. That ship had sailed a long long time ago. I was too wrapped up in club shit to do anything about it. I still wondered, though. What if she wouldn't have ever left town?

## 12

## Athena

"Hey, babe, wake up," Breaker whispered, tapping me on the shoulder. I felt like I'd slept for a week straight, my mouth tasting like straight-up sweaty ball sack, and my eyelids glued shut. I blinked them open, surprised that I could see out of both of them. My face was still a little sore, but it was obvious the swelling went down.

It was dark out, the air much colder than it was in Vegas, and I pulled my bathrobe tight as I sat up in the back of the truck. "Hey," I groaned. "Where are we?"

"Harrodsburg, Kentucky. You hungry? Thirsty?"

"I'm cold and I have to pee," I said, looking around the parking lot in front of the dingy motel. "Can you give me a minute?"

I slammed the truck door shut, my head pounding like a jackhammer was being drilled into my skull. I slipped into the sundress I brought with me and dug a hoodie out of my backpack to throw on top. *Fuck it*, I thought. This wasn't a fashion show. It was a kidnapping. These weren't men I was trying to impress. They were my brother's friends.

## Judas

Colt started pounding on the window, and I shot him a middle finger.

"Hurry up, sis," he shouted, as I slid out of the truck, finding my legs. My ankle still throbbed and my knees felt weak, but I wasn't about to show him I was struggling. I wasn't trying to throw off the damsel in distress vibe. Pissed-off porn star, however? That I could do.

"Where's my room?" I asked, holding out my hand for the key.

"Your room?" He laughed. "You're staying with me. Mom's orders. I'm not letting you out of my sight until I deliver you home in one piece."

"Mom's not here," I said, "and I don't even have fucking shoes, Colt. I'm not in a position to run off." I left the crew standing in the parking lot and wandered into the creepy little motel office. The man working the desk looked like a real treat, his greasy shoulder-length black hair and armpit stains proved hygiene wasn't one of his top priorities. His eyes were bloodshot red and a huge cloud of pot smoke lingered in the air. Made sense. This place was pretty desolate. He was probably bored.

"Holy shit," he stammered when he saw me, his jaw nearly hitting the desk. "You're…"

"Looking for a room?" I asked, finishing his sentence.

"No, no," he said. "I know you."

"No ya don't," I said.

"Don't play games with me, Athena," he said. "I know you. I watch your show every week. I'm your biggest fan."

"I don't know what you're talking about," I said with a shrug. I was really hoping this wasn't going to happen everywhere I went. I should've at least made the boys stop and grab me some hair dye before I went out in public. I was almost regretting not making Colt sleep on the floor of this nasty-ass place tonight just so I didn't have to talk to this guy. I pulled out a wad of cash from my backpack and slapped it on the counter. "I need a room."

"I'm gonna need a credit card," he said. "Just in case, damages and stuff. You probably know how it goes."

"I don't know how it goes," I said. "But whatever, here." I pulled out a prepaid cash card and slapped it down. "How much is it going to be?"

All I needed was a place to crash for a couple hours. This place was a complete shithole and this guy was making me nervous, the way his beady eyes were staring right through my clothes. I was used to that look, but in Vegas, I always had backup. Right now, I was alone and uncomfortable.

"For you? How does three hundred sound? I mean, unless you want to work something out." He reached across the counter and grabbed at my wrist, his fingers clamping down so tight I thought he was going to break my hand clean off.

"Hey!" I shouted. "Don't fucking touch me!"

Why the fuck was my pistol in my backpack and not on my hip?

The front door swung open and in swarmed the crew. I had never been so relieved and yet so humiliated at the same time. The man's eyes grew huge as Law's fist connected to his jaw.

"What do you think you're doing, my man?" Colt asked, standing over the grimy dude on the floor.

"I'm sorry, sir, I didn't realize she was with you," he said. "I'm sorry. It was nothing. Just, you know, who she is and everything. I thought my birthday came early."

"I'd shut that fucking mouth before you dug your hole any deeper," Law said, his boot hovering inches away from the guy's dick. "Where's the keys?"

The man motioned to the rack on the wall. "Room twelve is the nicest one," he said. "Just renovated."

"You been holding out on the good rooms?" Colt asked, his laugh twisted. "What the fuck, dude? I thought we were friends."

"I don't want no trouble," he pleaded.

"Leave him alone," I said, growing bored with the dick measuring contest going on in front of my face. I got it. They saved the day. Poor Princess Athena needed her big brother and his band of thugs to rescue her from this sweaty dude. "Here." I grabbed two more cash cards out of my backpack. "There should be three hundred between all of these." I tossed them on the floor next to where he laid, and Law handed me a key to room twelve. I stormed out of the office, the crew following behind me.

"Thank you," I said softly.

My brother looked at me with a type of compassion that I hadn't seen in a long time. "I know you can handle your own. You're just not playing with a full deck right now. I saw the way you limped in there. Like you said, you don't even have shoes. I'm sorry."

"I appreciate that," I said. I didn't know if I wanted to hug him or harm him. He was mostly the reason why I was in this position to begin with. "I need a hot shower. I'm going to my room."

*I didn't realize she was with you,* the man said. The sound of that simple sentence flooded me with memories of a time in my life where I was surrounded by men who would kill or be killed for me. Men who loved me just because I was born into the patch. It stirred a weird feeling inside my stomach. Was it regret? Or was I just being a sentimental baby. Surely a few days surrounded by the crew would remind me why I left in the first place.

If room twelve was the nicest in the motel, I felt bad for

the rest of the guys. The plaster on the wall was stained a nasty shade of brown and it reeked like a month-old ashtray. The carpet felt damp under my toes. The upside was somebody had left a half-drank bottle of whiskey on the nightstand. I picked it up and unscrewed the top, gagging into my mouth, the smell overpowering me. I tossed it across the room. That definitely wasn't whiskey. That was someone who was too lazy to go to the bathroom.

My hands were shaking. Was I in hell? I should've just taken my brother's advice and stayed with him. At least I'd have some company to commiserate with. This place was so disgusting, I didn't even want to think about peeling back the comforter to see what was under the sheets. Frustration overpowered me as I began to cry.

I stood perfectly still in the center of the room, bawling my eyes out, trying not to touch anything. What horrible life choice had I just made? I had been planning on running away from Vegas for forever, but was this what I got in return? This was nothing like the hot cowboy Montana fantasy I'd been playing over and over in my mind.

Even worse, I had stayed in places like this hundreds of times before. Before I got a little money and a little fame, this shit wouldn't have even fazed me. Had I really gotten that high-maintenance over the years? I was so conflicted.

I walked out into the parking lot, hoping I could figure out which room my brother was staying in. I watched as him and the rest of the crew got on their bikes and rode off, and sank my head into my hands. I should've just stuck with them. I wasn't in the mood to party, but maybe if I'd have gotten fucked-up enough, I wouldn't be so worried about the blood stains on the baseboards of the shitty hotel room.

"Hey," a voice called out in the darkness. I jumped, hoping it wasn't captain creepy. I looked over my shoulder, and it was Isaac, standing outside his room with his hands in his pockets.

"Oh hi," I said, avoiding his gaze. It was too familiar, but too strange. Kind of what I was craving but the generic knockoff version. Had his brother been here instead of him, I knew I'd be a lot better off. "Do you know where they went?"

"To town. Meeting up with the Debasers or some shit. I don't know. I'm on security detail." He pulled a cigarette out of his pocket and brought it to his lips.

"You got any more of those?" I asked. I didn't smoke, or at least I hadn't in a while, but if my life trajectory was going to look like this, I guess shaving a few years off my life wasn't the worst thing that could happen.

He passed me a smoke and lit it for me. I forgot how much I loved these things, the first hit going right to my head. He chuckled as he watched me.

"I'm sorry if I was being rude earlier," he said. "I never met someone famous before is all. I have a tendency to ramble when I'm nervous."

"It's alright," I said. "I wasn't exactly in my right mind myself. And I'm not famous. More like infamous."

"I feel like a moron," he said. "You gotta let me make it up to you."

"Oh, it's nothing," I said, stubbing out the cigarette on the side of the brick wall. "Don't worry about it."

"Come on. You gotta be hungry at least. Let's go find some food."

My stomach was growling. I had almost forgotten about the big greasy cheeseburgers I was fantasizing about a few short hours ago. "Yeah, I could do that. I don't want you to get in trouble, though. Aren't you supposed to be doing security?"

"I'm supposed to be making sure you don't run off," he said, chuckling. "You're not gonna make a break for it if I take you to the truck stop, are ya? I'm pretty sure Colt will murder me."

"If you take me to the truck stop you're probably going to have to carry me back out to the truck," I said with a laugh. "I couldn't tell ya the last time I had diner food." I debated a little bit with myself before getting in the truck. I didn't really like this guy. Never had. Even this afternoon, he rubbed me the wrong way, but out here in the darkness, it was a lot easier to pretend like he wasn't Isaac, the creepy kid who harassed me and my girlfriends. Underneath the street lamp, he almost looked like my old friend. Maybe I could just pretend.

"Have you talked to Judas at all since you moved away?" he asked, pulling out of the parking lot. I almost gasped. Were my thoughts that transparent?

"I haven't," I said, point-blank. "I haven't talked to anybody except my mama, to be honest. It's easier that way. Sometimes when you move away, you start getting sentimental, ya know? You start imagining things were better than when you left 'em." I wasn't sure why I was so willingly pouring my guts out to this guy, but it felt good saying it out loud. If I had a dollar for every time I almost gave up on my dreams and retreated back home, it'd probably fill up at least two backpacks as big as my other one.

"Well, you had to have at least wanted to come home a little bit. It wasn't like anybody held a gun to your head." I laughed nervously.

"Not to my head," I said. "What about poor Harold, though? Y'all know how to make an entrance, that's for sure."

"Poor Harold?" he asked, eyeing me sideways. Even this stranger could see through my bullshit.

"Listen, don't tell anybody, but I've been thinking about getting away for a while now. Not like this, obviously. I really really don't want to go home, though. I like being on my own."

"Fair enough."

When we got to the truck stop, I sent him into the convenience store to buy me a pair of flip-flops. The soles of my feet were filthy black. I'm sure the rest of me wasn't looking so hot either. I didn't care. If I couldn't have Montana, I was at least getting my cheeseburger.

We sat in a booth close to the door in the diner. Isaac might have just been a prospect, but he had all the mannerisms of the men I'd grown up with. He sat with one leg out of the booth, a clear view of anyone coming or going. It didn't matter that we were nowhere near home. You never knew when shit was going to hit the fan.

I pretended like I didn't notice. I pretended like I didn't care. Normalizing the club life was the only way to survive it. As long as my french fries were salty and this burger was medium rare, that was all I had to think about.

I wasn't trying to admit to myself the only thing I actually was thinking about was this man's brother. I wondered if he'd ever thought about me, or hell, if he even remembered me. He probably had a lot more on his plate than worrying about his best friend's porn star kid sister.

"Good thing Judas isn't here," Isaac said as I used my napkin to wipe up the cheeseburger disaster that was running down my arm. "He'd be side-eyeing you so hard right now."

I laughed, squeezing the fistful of beef. "He's still on that, huh? Good for him. How is he anyway?" I'm glad he brought up the subject so I wouldn't sound like such a creepy stalker. I loved that Judas was a vegetarian, even though I wasn't one myself. His commitment to his values just added this edge of dark sexiness to him. I liked a man who didn't compromise.

"He's not doing so hot, babe," he said. "His old lady is giving him a hard time. Drugs and shit."

His old lady. Of course he had an old lady. If he looked anything like he did back when we were growing up, he was probably swimming in old ladies. If the thought of him still made me feel some type of way even after all these years, I couldn't imagine being around him on a daily basis without wanting to rip his clothes off.

In that instant, I started tossing around an escape plan in my mind. It made me crazy knowing the only reason why I was willing to go back home was a man, and knowing that the fact he was accounted for was making me want to just hop in a random stranger's truck and tell them to take me west.

*You're being fucking crazy, Athena.*

"He's not doing drugs, is he?"

Isaac just shrugged. I couldn't believe he wouldn't eat chicken but he'd put a needle full of dope in his arm.

"I think that's why he wanted me to come prospect. Someone to keep him accountable. He's definitely been drinking a lot lately, but Betty Sue just got out of rehab, so who knows what happens next?"

I smiled a sad smile. Betty Sue. The junkie. *She sounded delightful.* I tried to envision in my mind what kind of woman he'd be with, what kind of woman it would take to turn the man who always had his shit together into an addict. I kind of always secretly hoped that if anyone was going to ruin his life, it'd be me. I didn't do drugs, but I definitely knew how to drive a man nuts.

"I think having you back will be good for him, to be

## Judas

honest. I wasn't supposed to tell you this, but he's the real reason why we came and got you. He's been telling your mom forever now that he's worried about you. Putting ideas in her head that you're not acting right on your show. He got her all worked up."

I dropped my cheeseburger mid-bite. I was going to throw up. My blood started to boil, but I couldn't decide if I was more angry or disgusted. What right did he have to tattle on me to my mom? What the fuck did he think he knew about me from watching me put on weekly sex shows? Why was he even watching?

It gave me the chills.

"I'm going to the bathroom," I said. "And next time you go to start a sentence with 'I wasn't supposed to tell you this,' you should probably think twice. You want to be a part of the MC, you need to learn to keep your fucking mouth shut, Isaac." I stormed off across the restaurant, shaking my head the entire time.

*Who the fuck did Judas think he was?* I slapped some cold water over my face, the familiar sting of tears beginning to well in my eyeballs. *If he wanted to save me, why didn't he chase after me? Why didn't he even try? I was just a kid back then... back when I needed him. Now I'm successful. I'm coveted. I'm powerful. Now, my life is none of his business. It's none of any of these guys' business.*

"Take me back to the motel," I said to Isaac as soon as I got back to the booth. I pulled some cash out of my backpack and slapped it on the table. I opened up my burner phone, trying to remember Harold's personal cell from the top of my head.

I wasn't going to let my brother and his crew control me. They had their chance a long time ago, and if they really cared about me, I would've been home a long time ago.

I was going to call Harold as soon as I figured out how. I could just frame this as a big misunderstanding and be on an airplane back to Vegas tomorrow. I'd waited this long to escape. A couple more months wasn't going to kill me.

The ride back to the motel was mostly silent. Isaac kept trying to explain away his blunder, telling me that maybe he misheard, and that I was blowing things out of proportion, but I wasn't trying to hear it. He needed to learn words couldn't be unsaid.

"Fuck my life," I muttered when we pulled into the dark parking lot and I caught the creepy clerk standing outside my door, hands in his pocket, fidgeting nervously. Could this night get any worse?

"You want me to handle it?" Isaac asked. I wanted to disappear was what I wanted. I didn't want him to think I needed him. Technically, I didn't. Still, it was late, and this guy had already proven himself a creep.

He rolled down the truck window and shouted, "Can I help you, man?"

The guy leapt nearly three feet in the air. I knew Isaac was just a lowly prospect, but the creep didn't have to know that.

"I'm not gonna hurt you, buddy," he said. "I just want to know what you're doing outside the lady's room."

"Do you know where she is?" he asked. Against my better judgment, I peeked over Isaac's shoulder.

"What the hell do you want?" I barked. I was used to crazy. Some guys wouldn't take no for an answer. I figured a boot in his face fixed him up right quick, but apparently he was not that easy to shake. "I thought we told you!"

"Ma'am," he said sheepishly. He was holding the cash cards I paid him with. "I can't take these. They're too much."

"Keep 'em," I said. "It's no big deal." I sank back into

the seat of the truck and sighed. If he thought he was going to win me over giving me *back* my money, he was more than just delusional.

"No, seriously," he said, approaching the truck, holding his hands up in the air. "I think there's a mistake. These cards are worth ten thousand dollars apiece. I can't take that."

"Wait, what now?" I stammered. My heart stopped. I could feel the blood draining from my face. "I think you're confused. That can't be right."

"I thought so, too," he said. "I went to cash them at the ATM, though. I tried 'em all. All the same."

"Gimme those!" Isaac said, yanking them from his hand.

That couldn't be right. When I set up the software to hack the accounts, it was only supposed to take a maximum of one hundred dollars, in slow unnoticeable increments. Anything more than that was a dangerous game. Anything more than that would definitely get me caught. Sure, I was very careful about setting up an untraceable business to do my dirty deeds, but I figured if I ever got caught, I could explain things away as an accident. Ten thousand dollars was no accident. Ten thousand dollars was the kind of money that could get a girl killed.

In an instant, I went from being on the run by choice to being on the run. My backpack wasn't full of petty cash anymore. It was full of chunks of money that even the rich and dangerous men I pilfered it from would easily notice. They were the kind of people who could afford to do digging. They were the kind of people who weren't afraid to ask questions or do whatever it took to make criminals like me disappear. This wasn't a joke anymore. It wasn't a game. This was my life on the line, and the only people I had to rely on were the men in the very club that I spent my life trying to get away from.

"We gotta go," I managed to stammer to Isaac, trying to gather my thoughts. "This is not good."

"You're kidding, right?" he asked. "How many of those you got?"

I didn't want to think about it. "Seriously, Isaac. We can't stay here any longer. We aren't safe." I thought about all the people who had seen me in the short amount of time we spent here in Kentucky. Maybe I was being overly paranoid, but I could've sworn people at the truck stop were looking at me like they knew me. Then there was this guy, this creeper, who had full-blown confirmation it was me. I reached in the glove box instinctively, knowing full well the pistol would be there, still relieved as I palmed it in my hand. I pointed it right at the clerk.

He raised his hands into the air and began to walk back slowly.

"Please, Miss Athena, I swear, I saw nothing. I don't know anything. I was just trying to be a good guy. You gotta believe me. I don't want no trouble." The truth was, I did believe him. I didn't think for one second he would throw me under the bus, merely because his giving me the cards back meant he wasn't motivated by money. No, this man wanted to impress me.

"I'm not going to hurt you," I said. "I just need you to know how serious I am right now." My hands were trembling, the gun drooping up and down. If I tried to shoot it, I'd probably end up blowing a hole in the roof of the truck or rearranging Isaac's face. "There might be some people coming here looking for me in the next few days. I need you to do me a huge favor."

"I never saw you, I swear," he said. "You were never here."

## Judas

"No," I said. These men coming to look for me weren't the kind who would accept that as a logical answer. They'd torture it right out of him. As sleazy as he was, I wouldn't wish my shit upon anyone. "I was here. Can you remember a phone number?"

He nodded, his eyes wide with fear as I rattled off the number to one of my burner phones. "Tell them that's the number I left when I checked in."

"Got it," he said. I put the gun back in the glove compartment and he relaxed, slinking over to my side of the truck. "So what do I get out of this?"

"How about not killed and disappeared?" Isaac asked, reaching for his holster.

"Stop," I said. I slid my panties down my thighs and tossed them out the window right into the clerk's hand. "Thanks for your hospitality... I never caught your name."

"Steve," he said with a chuckle, clutching the lacy red underwear in his hand.

"It was a pleasure to meet you, Steve. I hope next time I see you it isn't under such distressing circumstances." Isaac rolled his eyes and made a fake gagging sound. I rolled up my window and turned to him. "Take me back to the truck stop."

"What the hell is going on, woman?" he asked.

"We're going home a little early," I said. "But first, I need to take this phone and drop it in the back of a random truck." It might not completely solve my problem, but it would at least give me some time to think.

"I can't," he said. "I only answer to Colt."

"Get him on the phone," I said. "He wants his sister back with the crew? This is what he gets. Now drive, Isaac, or trade me spots."

"Just so you know, you can't pull that panties shit on me," he muttered as he pulled out of the parking lot. "I'd never cave for some broad's g-string. Fucking pathetic loser."

I giggled, shrugging my shoulders. He was exactly the kind of man who would sing like a bird for a pair of used panties, but I'd let him hold on to his ego, at least until he got me back to the clubhouse. "That's good," I said, raising my eyebrows, "because I don't have any more at the moment. Now get my brother on the phone."

# 13

## Judas

The pounding on my door shook me out of my dead slumber. I instinctively reached for my pistol on the nightstand, flipping on my lamp and letting my eyes adjust to the bright light. Never a dull moment around here, even when everyone was out of town.

"Judas!" the familiar whine of Betty Sue drifted from the other side of the door. "Are you in there?" I groaned and pulled my blankets back up over my body and rolled over. I didn't feel like dealing with this bitch right now. "Please!" she said, pounding harder. "It's an emergency."

I looked at the clock on the nightstand. 4 a.m. I needed to be awake and functional again in an hour for dumpster pick up.

"Come back in an hour," I said. "I'm busy."

"You got a bitch in there?" she shouted. It was none of her business either way. We were done for over a year now. The only reason I kept her around was because I felt guilty. I brought her into this life, I wrecked her. The least I could do was try and help her get her shit together. Not at 4 a.m., though.

"Yeah," I said, hoping that would scare her off. I smashed my face into the pillow and tried to drown out her incoherent whining.

"I know you don't, you asshole. Why are you trying to be cruel to me? You know I'm fragile right now." She wasn't just knocking anymore. Now she was kicking. I knew she'd never get through the stainless steel door, but she was irritating the shit out of me now. I got out of bed and slid on a pair of sweatpants. I unlocked the door and only opened it a crack, bracing it tight so she couldn't just sneak on in.

"What do you want?" I asked. "Why are you up? Why are you here? You're supposed to be at the halfway house. Don't you have curfew and shit?"

"Stop," she said, driving her palm into the door, trying to push it open. "You're giving me a headache." I could tell by her sway she was obviously on something. Her big blue eyes were nearly bulging out of her head. I used to think they were so pretty; I could get lost in them hours and hours while we laid together in bed. Now, her eyes made me anxious, always darting around like she was paranoid about something. Nothing about her was pretty to me anymore. Not the way she looked, not the way she acted, especially not the way she made me feel. "Just let me in. I want to talk to you."

"We can talk right here," I said. "You know you're not allowed in here anymore."

Not since the incident.

We'd tried to work things out. I was even willing to put up with her constant verbal assaults and the idea that the rest of our life would consist of me trying to help her not to relapse. When she started fucking Isaac, though, there was no more working things out.

I'd never be able to get hard for her again, knowing

that my brother was inside her. I could never look at her like the beautiful woman I fell in love with all those years ago knowing she was that willing to betray me just for a temporary fix. It was just one of those double standards. I could forgive Isaac for just about anything, as proven time and time again, but I didn't deal with cheating old ladies. I'd been burned enough times by people I trusted.

"I don't understand why you won't just get off it," she said. "You know I wasn't in my right mind. You know that wasn't me. It was the drugs. I'm clean now," she said, those big blue eyes not even trying to make contact with mine.

"What do you want, Betty Sue? You need money? I'll get my wallet. Let me put some clothes on and I'll take you back to where you need to go." Paying her off and making her disappear was always the easiest option.

She nodded before cupping her head in her hands. This broken woman standing before me, thin as a rail, white as a sheet, just a shell of the person I once loved, I couldn't find it in me to just slam the door in her face, even though I knew that was the smartest thing to do.

She followed behind me into my room against my better judgment. Before I could pull a pair of jeans out of my dresser, she was laying across my bed.

"I'll suck your dick if you let me stay here," she said. "Just for the day."

"No," I said. "I'm fucking busy. I have to go to work. I don't have time to keep an eye on you. You know I don't want you, Betty Sue. I'd rather stick my dick in a cactus than anywhere near you. Get up. I'm taking you back to your place."

"Come on, Judas. I can't go back there now. I'm already in deep shit for missing curfew. Let me at least have a couple hours to get my story together. If I go back now, they'll throw me in jail."

"Jail's not so bad," I said, starting a pot of coffee. It didn't look like I was going to get any more sleep today before work. I went into the bathroom to take a piss and brush my teeth, and when I came back into my bedroom, she was passed out across the top of the comforter, mouth wide open, snoring like a chainsaw.

"Whatever," I muttered to myself. The only thing I could hope was that she'd be gone again before I got back from work. Maybe she'd find someone else who wanted to listen to her sob story. I had dumpsters to tend to, one of the least glamorous parts of the job, but one of the most lucrative, too. I filled my thermos with coffee and tried to be as quiet as possible as I stepped out of my room, cringing at the way the door creaked shut behind me.

The hallway was dark, the clubhouse was dead, and I hoped by the time I got back my crew would be home. It was eerie being here without them. The silence reminded me too much of back when I was growing up. I was so alone in the world. The MC gave me a family, a life, loud noises and chaos, enough overwhelming shit that I didn't have time to be alone with my thoughts. I didn't have time to dwell on the sad shit I'd been through.

I pulled the dump truck out of the garage, the smell of diesel burning in the air, thick clouds of smoke pouring up into the clear morning sky. I put my black coffee to my lips, wiping the sleep out of my eyes, thankful the prospects would be back to do this tomorrow. I'd graduated a long time ago from the ranks of garbageman. Driving this truck brought back some real wild memories of Colt and me, two teenage boys who thought we were kings of the world getting to drive his daddy's dump truck.

As I drove down the long dirt road that led to my route, I could've sworn I passed the big red truck and trailer the guys hauled out to Vegas. It was dark, though, and I was still half asleep and half worried about what the hell Betty Sue getting kicked out of her halfway house was going to entail. It was probably just wishful thinking on my part. I pulled my good morning joint from my pocket and fired it up.

# 14

## Athena

"Where are you gonna stay?" Isaac asked me as we sat in the idling truck in front of the clubhouse. "Nobody's up. You just want to come to my house for a little bit until the guys get back in town?"

I didn't know how he got the impression that I wanted really anything to do with him. He was an easy getaway ride. The only reason why I stayed awake the whole drive back here and talked to him was because I was afraid if I fell asleep, something creepy would happen. He was annoying as hell, overly confident for no apparent reason. If I had to hear one more time about how he fucked his brother's old lady, I was going to open the door and push him out onto the highway. If my dad was still around, that guy would've never made it past hang-around. Hell, he'd probably be missing some body parts by now, the way he ran his mouth. Colt really needed to tighten things up if he was going to keep this club functional. Why the fuck did I care, though? I definitely wasn't going to be able to stick around for long.

"I'm fine," I said to him. To be honest, I wasn't sure

how it was going to feel walking through those doors for the first time after all these years. I never lived at the clubhouse, but the amount of time I spent there growing up was more time than I spent in my house. In some ways, it was more etched into my soul than my actual home. So many memories, good and bad. So many turning points in my life, like the first time I caught my dad cheating on my mom, or the first time I saw someone bleed to death on a concrete floor. My first beer. My first kiss. "I kind of want to be by myself for a little bit. Thanks for the ride."

"I'm going to see you around, right?" he asked.

"Sure," I said, grabbing my stuff and getting out of the truck. The sun was just starting to come up over the mountains, a sight I didn't realize how much I had missed. The air was wet, cool and crisp, and just standing out in front of the gaudy yellow aluminum-sided building made me feel like I stepped into a time machine. Everything looked the same. The faint smell of diesel fuel was in the air, the gravel kicked up dust as he drove off, and the way the wooden steps on the porch groaned under my feet was exactly the way I remembered it. I was overwhelmed. This humble little shack was nothing like the places I'd lived since I ran away, but it felt more real than any of the fancy apartments or hotels or mansions I'd laid my head. The hair on my arm stood up as I imagined the vision of my father and his men lined up at the bar on the other side of the door. I knew it was impossible.

I could almost hear the wails of my mother when she found out what happened at the strip club that night. I could feel the collective sadness of all the old ladies and sluts gathered around the room, mourning their beloveds. The rage of my brother and the other survivors burned so hot, it felt like everyone was going to spontaneously combust at any minute. I was suffocating, just a dumb seventeen-year-old with a nice set of legs and an unhealthy daddy complex, looking to run off with the first man who paid attention to me. I bailed because of how hard it was to be here in the aftermath.

It was still hard.

I felt like a little girl again, peeking in the windows, not knowing what I was going to find on the other side of the wall. I felt my posture shrink, like I wanted to disappear all over again. They wanted me here, but why?

No signs of movement inside, I took a deep breath and pulled on the door. I was relieved it swung right open, albeit confused. Since when was everyone so careless?

The rising sun shined just enough through the window blinds to softly light up the barroom. It looked exactly like I left it: the huge Indignant flag hanging on the wall, wooden barstools, and couches scattered throughout, the hardwood floor scuffed from years and years of dirty boots. Cheap perfume and cigar smoke wafted through the air, along with the smell of stale spilled beer. *What a dump.* These men might run a garbage business, but at least they could keep their hangout clean. What the hell were prospects for these days anyway?

I was jolted from my exploration by the sound of snoring coming from one of the couches. A woman's voice murmured incoherent babble. I'd know that voice anywhere, even after being away for so long.

"Tressica," I whispered into the dark. "Is that you?"

"What?" she groaned. "Oh fuck me, what time is it?" I ran over to the nearby couch, squatting down next to my longtime high school friend. Last I'd heard, she went off to college to become a lawyer. What she was doing slumming it here was beyond me.

She looked pretty as ever even in her state of confused slumber. Her wild blonde hair looked like a mane, crimped and curled, and her smeared lipstick and running eyeliner didn't detract from the delicate features of her face. She was built, tall, strong, curvy, her feet hanging off the edge of the couch. The sweatshirt she was using as a blanket barely covered her nearly naked torso.

"Hey," she said, smiling from ear to ear when she realized who she was face-to-face with. "Oh my God, Athena, I'm so happy to see you." She grumbled a little as she threw her arms around me. I hadn't been hugged like that in as long as I could remember. Not the cordial kiss on the cheek type of hug, the genuine kind, the kind that only a true friend was capable of. I'd only been back for moments, and already I was being sucked right back in.

"Tress, I'm so happy to see you, too, but what are you doing here?"

The overhead lights flicked on, startling us both, and I slapped my hands over my eyes.

"Rise and shine!" my mother shouted. "Who's ready for some hair of the dog?"

"Mom…" I stammered, watching her clank liquor bottles around behind the bar. "What are you doing?"

"Hey, baby," she said, her big warm smile exactly how I remembered it. Mostly everything else about her looked older, from the wrinkles on her neck to the gray in her hair, but the tight black tank top and skinny jeans she was wearing proved that her body was still as firm as it was when she was in her twenties. "I'm fixing breakfast. You want?"

She pulled out a bottle of Bloody Mary mix and I shrugged. It wasn't even 7 a.m. and I was deliriously tired, but a drink would probably knock me out hard enough right now that I'd be snoring like Tressica in two minutes flat. I needed to rest before I plotted my next move anyway.

"You're not going to hug me?" I asked.

"Honey, I'm scared I'll break you in half. You're skin and bones other than those airbags, and I know for a fact those aren't factory issued." She slid a glass across the bar, eyeing me suspiciously. So much for a mother's love. She was always quick to pick, especially about my appearance. I didn't know why I thought time might've changed her. "How about you, Tress? You ready to keep the party going?"

"I gotta go to work," she said. "but I'll be back tonight. I want to catch up, Athena. I've missed you so much." She scurried out the door before I even had a chance to say goodbye, and I could tell something was off just by the way she walked. Tressica had always been a shoulders back, head high kind of girl, but something about her looked squished. Sad. Like all the other club sluts doing their morning walk of shame.

"Who's she banging?" I asked as soon as the door shut behind her.

"Your brother," she said.

"What? No… what about Zelda?"

"Oh, she's still in the picture. I don't think Zelda knows about the severity of the situation, but I tried my best last night to get 'em nice and liquored up so I could watch them scrap it out. Tress held strong though. She really should've finished law school. She lies better than any lawyer I've ever met."

"You're sick," I said.

"Hey, I gotta get my kicks somehow. With the boys out of town, there isn't a lot of entertainment around here." She took a long swig from her drink, which was definitely more vodka than tomato juice, and I rolled my eyes at her.

"Why don't you get a hobby or something? Aren't you

a little old to be running around with bikers and day drinking?"

"And aren't you a little whorish to be judging people's life choices?" she asked with a wink. She poked me square in the nose. "How much did that set you back?"

"You're a bitch," I said.

"I missed you, sweetie." She stroked her fingers through my hair and cupped my chin in her hand. "I don't care how many people have seen your ass on the internet; to me, it will always be my cute little baby bum. I'm really glad to have you home."

Classic Reena. You never knew when she was being cruel or being kind. You never knew if she genuinely cared or if she was just getting you buttered up so she could rip out your beating heart.

"This isn't my home, Mom. I'm just here for a minute. I have some business I need to take care of and then I have to move on."

"Right, right," she said. She topped off her glass with vodka.

"What are you doing here so early anyway? Why aren't you at the house?"

"Oh, honey, I sold the house years ago. It was too lonely being there all by myself with you and your brother gone and your daddy dead. I didn't need all that. I live here now. Makes it a lot easier to keep an eye on the boys, make sure they're clean and fed. When is everybody getting back? I should probably start breakfast."

Weird. Growing up, my mom never had a maternal bone in her body. She could barely keep Colt and I clean and fed because she was too busy worrying about who and what my dad was doing. Maybe she was making up for lost time. Maybe she was just hoping another husband would fall in her lap so she could go back to the only life she knew. It was sad, bordering pathetic. My mother was a beautiful, bold woman and was basically reduced to a live-in maid for a bunch of outlaws. I was definitely going to do whatever I could to not follow in her footsteps.

"Well I guess I'm going to go find a spare bedroom to crash in since I don't have a house anymore."

"Here," she said, tossing me a set of keys. "Nobody ever took Rubin's old room. You're more than welcome." Poor Rubin. He was always one of my favorite men, a little weird, a little quiet, and definitely completely misunderstood by the world. The club was all he had. He didn't die that day in the strip club, but the guilt ate him up so bad he drove his bike off the Main Street bridge three days later. Had a backpack full of cinder blocks strapped to his back. It was just another testament to the fact that you die by the patch one way or another. Just another reason why I wanted no part of this life, even if mine was a complete mess.

"Is it still full of snakes and porn magazines?"

"Oh no, honey," she said with a giggle. "We found good homes for all the snakes. I don't know what happened to the porn magazines, but I can probably find them if you want to go through them and look for pictures of your friends so you don't feel lonely."

I shot her a middle finger and headed for the hallway. When I was a kid, I knew better than to ever walk through that swinging door that separated the clubhouse from the living quarters. It was basically a dormitory for deadbeats, a den of filth, a corridor of anything goes. The one time I went back there looking to bum a smoke off of Colt, my twelve-year-old eyes saw more than they could process when I walked past a room and locked eyes with a woman pleading for her life as my father and his friends were impaling her body.

## Judas

It was a turning point for me. A vision I could never shake. It didn't matter that she kept hanging around the club after that. It was part of the reason why I went into the porn business to begin with. Nobody was going to do stuff to me like that unless I signed up for it. No man would ever take my power from me like the MC did with these women. No one would ever leave me without a soul like my mother.

I got chills as I passed that room.

Three doors down was another room that gave me a different kind of chills.

Judas's old room. When he got out of jail he moved right into the clubhouse. The men took him in quickly, probably because they knew his history of darkness and wanted them to be a part of their army. They wanted to groom him to be just like them. He was always just 'different' though. Even in his youth, he had this quiet dark power about him. Nobody ever went in his room unless it was by strict invitation. He kept things so neat and tidy to the point of sterile, clinical. It made me sad thinking that the place he was most comfortable his whole life was in a jail cell, judging by the way he kept his room. Everything had a place. He obsessively vacuumed. He never let the sluts clean up after him like most of the other men did. His space was sacred.

I lingered outside his room for a minute, and I swore I could smell him. It was likely my brain playing tricks on me, but the earthy fragrance, like the aftermath of a thunderstorm, rushed over me. I wondered if he was in there, sleeping. I ran my palm up and down the stainless steel door, trying to feel for something on the other side. A sign. A reason to pop my head in and get a glimpse of this man who supposedly never gave up on me, even after all these years.

I got my sign loud and clear as the door swung open and a bug-eyed brunette popped her head out into the hallway.

"Can I help you?" she asked. I jumped a little before composing myself. Even with this broad standing in the doorway, I couldn't resist peeking over her, trying to catch a glimpse of what his life looked like now beyond the pockmarked face of a girl I assumed was Betty Sue. "Excuse me?" she said impatiently.

"Sorry," I said. "I was just looking for Rubin's old room. Haven't been back this way in a while. I kinda got lost." His room was exactly how I remembered it, nothing remotely out of place except the crumpled up comforter where she was likely sleeping.

"Oh." She shrugged. "Is anybody out there?"

"Just my mom," I said. "Er... I mean, Reena."

"Shit," she stammered. "I thought you looked familiar. It's nice to actually meet you. My man seems to be a really big fan of yours. Is that gonna be a problem?" Even though she was standing right in my face, trying to make herself big and threatening, I knew I could probably poke her between the eyes and she'd drop to the ground. My momma thought I looked frail? This bitch looked like she was on a strict diet of dick and meth.

"It's not going to be a problem at all," I said. I meant it, too. Never in my life would I fight for a man. I didn't need to take what wasn't mine, and I sure as hell wasn't trying to settle down here.

"I mean, his birthday is coming up. Maybe we could arrange something... just the three of us?" I tried not to throw up in my mouth.

"I don't think you have that kind of money laying around," I said, trying to sugarcoat my disgust. "I'm flattered though."

"Whatever. Your loss." I watched as she felt the locks on the other side of the door before jiggling the handle to make sure it was locked. She slammed it shut, and for some reason, that stuck in my mind. If they were that serious, why didn't she have a key of her own?

Maybe she lost it. Maybe she got confused and put it in her crack pipe and smoked it. I didn't know what the purpose of hanging on to any thread of hope was. He and I were nothing. We'd never be anything. I definitely didn't belong here.

Maybe I'd mistaken his alleged concern for me according to Isaac for the way that most men saw me. A fun fantasy, but not something you'd want every day. Girls like Betty Sue were for every day. I was just the third wheel. At least I used to be.

Now that part of me was dead.

Dead like the smell coming out from underneath Rubin's door. *How had nobody noticed this?* It was probably one of his many pet snakes. Probably one got loose and wedged itself somewhere and nobody cared enough to find it. I turned the key in the lock, and as I opened the door, the smell overpowered me to the point of gagging. I screamed at the top of my lungs and took off running down the hallway as fast as I could when I spotted the creature there, snapping his jaws as he thrashed around in the little plastic pool.

"What the fuck?!" I shouted as I barreled into my mother, damn near knocking her to the ground.

She threw her head back and cackled like a witch as I stood before her trembling. "I see you met our mascot."

*A live fucking alligator. Of course these idiots would have a live alligator.*

"You're a bunch of goddamn morons," I muttered.

"Oh come on, he's kind of cute once you get to know

him," she said. "Delaney just fed him last night. He's probably in a great mood."

"Fuck you, Mom," I muttered. I was beyond exhausted, but I sure as hell wasn't sticking around for any more of her strange games. The Terryton Motel was close enough to walk. I stormed toward the front door, but the large figure standing in the way stopped me in my tracks. I looked up slowly, soaking in his broad chest, his wide shoulders, the dark stubble on his chin. The second I looked into his eyes, I had to look away. I couldn't breathe. I couldn't speak.

"Athena?" he asked, shaking his head and wiping his eyes.

I nodded, gulped, and stared at my feet. I didn't know what to say. This voice in my head was telling me to run, but my legs felt like they were full of cement.

"You gonna be around for a while?" he asked. The way he brushed past me and walked off brought me back to reality. His tone was cold and casual, and I didn't even think he cared if I answered.

"I don't know," I said.

"Alright," he said, shrugging, walking off toward the hallway. I stormed out the front door, more confused than I was when I started on this adventure. More than ever, I knew I needed to get away.

# 15

## Isaac

So maybe Betty Sue's lips were wrapped around my dick as I drove down the back roads, but I couldn't get Athena off my mind. I was trying to be a gentleman, trying not to hit any potholes for the sake of her jaw, but I couldn't stop thinking about that hot blonde that was just in the passenger seat a few hours ago.

I could tell Athena liked me. Why else would she have stayed up all night talking with me? Stealing her right out from under Judas was going to be awesome. Just like I did with this dumb bitch.

"Where you supposed to be?" I asked her. I knew she was staying at the halfway house one town over. She'd been blowing my phone up all night asking when I was getting back into town. I obviously didn't respond. This bitch was clingy, and I didn't want to give her the wrong idea.

"What do you mean?" she asked, gasping for air and wiping the drool off her chin as she looked up at me.

"Aw, don't stop, babe," I groaned. I was so close.

"You asked me a question, you idiot," she said. "I

thought we had an arrangement. I thought I was coming to stay at your place for a while."

I brushed her hair out of her eyes, abruptly grabbing for the back of her head and sliding her back down onto my throbbing cock. She sputtered and groaned but got right back to work like the dirty slut she was. She was definitely not coming to stay at my place for a while. Not ever.

"I never that said," I moaned as I worked her mouth up and down my shaft, down so hard she began to gag. "You need to lay off the drugs." She tried to pull away, struggled with all her might, and the instant I felt her teeth graze my dick, I pulled out, backhanding her across the face.

I didn't know what was sexier, her crying or the way she gagged and sputtered, but my cock exploded, just like that, coating my sweatshirt in a sticky film.

"Look what you made me do, bitch." I laughed through my moans. She wasn't amused, gripping the side of her face like I'd actually hurt her. "I've hit you harder before and you liked it."

"You're a piece of shit. If I'd have known what kind of guy you were, I would've never fucked you in the first place. You're no better than your asshole brother." She hung her head in her hands and began to full-blown bawl. It definitely wasn't sexy anymore. Now it was just needy, clingy. It wasn't supposed to end up like this. I just wanted Judas to walk in on the two of us together and snap. I wanted an excuse to take him out once and for all in an act of self-defense.

Instead, he was his usual stoic self: steady, rational, accepting the situation and moving on like it was no big thing. Judas didn't snap anymore, though. Not since that time on the farm when we were teenagers. Ever since he got out of jail he was calm all the time. There was nothing

## Judas

I could do to get him angry like he did when we were kids. I figured even asking to join the club would send him into a wild fit after everything I'd done to him, but instead he welcomed me back in like a brother, open arms, treating me like nothing had ever happened. It wasn't right. It was strange. Probably just his way of always showing me he was better than me. He was always the favored twin even if he got in the most trouble. Hell, even before our parents died, I knew they loved him more than me. The only way anyone would've paid attention to me as a teenager was if I put him in jail. And that fucker forgave me.

Now I was stuck with little miss meth-head following me around like a puppy dog. Maybe if she actually was a puppy dog he'd give a fuck. This obviously wasn't working. She had to go.

"Take me back to the clubhouse right now," she said. "I need to get cleaned up." I didn't even think about that. If I was going to dump her in the woods I definitely needed to take care of the DNA situation she had going on. If I learned anything from being in the club it was not to leave a trace of evidence behind. My brother and his men were masters at cleanup, the reason why I always kept a kit in my truck.

I turned down a road that cut back into the woods.

"Where are we going, Isaac?" she asked. "I don't know this shortcut."

Her phone started to ring, and before I could grab it out of her hand, she answered it.

"Hey, Judas," she said dramatically. "Just out for a ride. No, I swear I didn't take your watch. I think you were wearing it this morning." She pulled a gold Rolex from her purse and dangled it in front of my face. "I'm not coming back," she said. "I'm out with a friend. Don't *babe* me; I'm tired of your shit."

She hung up the phone, turning to me with a scandalous smile on her face. That right there was the thing about her that turned me on the most, her willingness to feed into the destruction of my brother. He obviously still had a little something for her or he wouldn't be calling her up looking for her. If he didn't care, he'd have just let her walk away and never said a word to her again. I knew the way he operated.

I was glad I didn't have to kill this bitch today. She was fucking annoying, but it was pretty easy to shut her up, either with my fists or some drugs. When she was damn near catatonic she was kind of pretty. Every time I stuck my dick in her I felt like I was fucking my brother a little bit harder. I'd save her for a rainy day.

"Seriously, Isaac, where are we going?" she asked as I stopped my truck, backing it up into a little divot where the trees cleared just enough that nobody could see us parked. "Are you gonna fucking kill me?"

"Not today," I said with a shrug. I cupped her chin in my hand and kissed her on the lips. "I gotta take a piss. Stay here."

# 16

## Judas

I was dead exhausted after a morning on the road all by myself.

All I could think about the whole time was what the fuck Betty Sue could possibly be up to in my room. If she overdosed there, I wasn't sure what I'd do. I forgot to hide my watch, the last thing I still had from my parents' estate, an heirloom passed all the way down from my great-granddaddy. I forgot I basically had to nail everything to the floor whenever she came around or it'd be gone.

I was tired. I stank like a garbage truck. My body ached from standing on the concrete all day yesterday. I was getting too old for this shit. Then I saw her there, standing in the doorway, looking like a woman who had nothing left to lose.

Her face was red, and up close she looked a lot thinner than she did online. Her clothes were wrinkled, eyes were puffy, and still she was the prettiest thing I'd ever seen. I was so overwhelmed by Athena's presence back in the house I fucking blew it.

Walked off like I didn't give a fuck. Brushed past her

before I could process just how cut up I felt just by the sight of her. If this was the 'present' Colt had promised me the night before, she didn't look too thrilled. She had that look of leaving, that look she always had, like being in this house sucked all the life right out of her fragile body. Who was I to stop her.

I ran to my room, and Betty Sue was gone. I figured as much. Did a security check and, lo and behold, the bitch grabbed my watch. She didn't take my pistol, to my relief. I would've definitely had to track her down. I called her up and tried to make nice for the sake of my granddad's watch, and of course she lied about taking it. I'd just have to show my face at the local pawn shops this afternoon to make sure nobody bought that shit.

I got in the shower, blasting myself with cold water, trying to cool my temper, but I just found myself more and more frustrated. Not at Betty Sue. She was a club slut and she'd always be a club slut.

I was pissed at myself. How in the ever-loving fuck did I just graze past Athena like it wasn't even a thing? How did I let that sad broken girl just walk out the door? I let her go once, but back then it wasn't my place to say anything. I felt so bad about the shit she saw growing up in the club. I figured anywhere she went was better than here.

Now?

*It's none of your fucking business. If she wanted to talk, she would've followed you.*

I tried to remind myself of old Athena, the wild child who could never be told what to do. I remember the first time I stepped in between her and this little punk bitch who thought it was cute to put his hands on her. She wouldn't speak to me for two months. The first time I told her I thought he wasn't that bad, she promptly broke up with him and sent Colt and me over to his house to shake him up a little bit.

Games. Athena was all about mind games. She fucked with my head then, and she was fucking with my head now. We had some shit to straighten out, and I needed to stop her before she got away again.

I toweled myself off quickly and threw on some jeans and a t-shirt. I slapped a bandana around my head and grabbed my jacket. I sprinted to the garage, hoping she didn't make it too far, and fired up my blacked-out Harley Iron 883. The morning sun was bright, and I pulled my sunglasses down over my eyes. I didn't have to drive too far before I saw her; hell, if I would've pulled out of the parking lot I would've missed her. She was sitting on the front porch of the clubhouse, a cigarette hanging from her lips, looking like she was half asleep. She jumped up from the rocking chair as I pulled closer, looking around like someone had just detonated a bomb.

"Jesus Christ, what kind of exhaust you got on that fucking thing?" she shouted.

I shrugged. Athena never paid much mind to motorcycles. She thought men who rode them were trying to make up for the size of their dicks, and women who rode them were just trying to impress those men. I never had the chance to show her, not my dick, even though she'd probably be pleasantly surprised, but the freedom that getting on a motorcycle could bring. The power it brought, not just because of how folks looked at a man on a motorcycle, but because all alone out there on the road, you were staring death in the face every second and telling it to fuck off, or in the case of some guys, bring it on. She'd learn to love it if she had the chance.

"You need a ride somewhere?" I asked, letting my engine idle.

"Why'd you do that?" she asked. I slid up my sunglasses and raised my eyebrow.

"I didn't do anything," I said. "You were on your way out. Again. Not my place to stop you."

"Judas, I know why Colt brought me here. I'd at least think you'd give me a proper hello."

"I don't know what you're talking about," I said. Sure, I might've casually dropped some comments to Colt and Reena about how she hadn't been acting right lately, but I never once said I was trying to fix her. Seeing her here in front of me made me want nothing more than to scoop her up in my arms and lock her in my room, do whatever it took to make her happy again, but that wasn't my style. I could forgive and forget, but Lord knew I couldn't make anyone better. Betty Sue was a prime example.

"Okay," she said, rolling her eyes. "Well, don't let me hold you back from whatever you're doing. I'm just gonna take a nap and wait for the rest of the guys to get back." She grabbed her knees and sank back into the chair, closing her eyes.

"You ran off. You left us all when we needed you," I muttered.

"I needed stability, Judas. I needed to be around people who weren't completely fucked-up." She looked like I'd slapped her. I spat on the gravel and slid my sunglasses back down. I tried to bite my tongue, but I'd been waiting a long time to get this off my chest.

"People who weren't completely fucked-up? You ran off with a pedophile and started a porn business. Were we really that bad to you, Athena?"

She closed her eyes again, sinking back into the chair, her white blonde hair cascading down over her eyes as she curled her plump lips into a straight line.

## Judas

"You can go sleep in my room if you want," I said. "Bugs will eat you alive out here."

"Is that part of your sick plan? Your old lady already tried to get me in bed once this morning."

"I don't have an old lady," I said.

"Whatever." She yawned and stretched her arms over her head. Her face was so cute pinched up like that. Everything about her in her natural state was cute, even if every part on her body was so unnatural, like a caricature of the girl I once knew. She needed to put on some weight. I wasn't sure how her frame supported those big old bolt-ons. I didn't dislike them by any means, but I'm sure her back hurt all the time. "You, personally, Judas, you were never that bad to me. You were always very good to me. You looked out for me even when I didn't want you to. You weren't the club, though. You weren't my family. You were just an ex-con who my brother was friends with."

"Well, I am the club now, Athena. I'm the vice-president of this club, and I take my job seriously. I am your family even if you don't want me to be. And if you want to split hairs, my record was wiped when I turned eighteen. Fuck off with your outdated nomenclature."

"Exactly," she said. "You are the club now. I hate how you look in those leathers. You got your record wiped and decided to start working on another one? I expected so much more from you."

As much as I wanted to explain to her how different things were now that Colt and I ran the roost, I wasn't going to waste my breath on someone who didn't even want to be here. She could judge me all she wanted, but when she started throwing ideas around like they were facts, insulting my choices when she had absolutely zero right to, that's when I just shut down. Not worth my breath. Not worth my anger. I saved that for those who understood the atrocities they'd committed.

Just then, I caught the low hum of Colt's exhaust coming down the road, the pause of his idling motor as he unlocked the gate that led up to the house. The rumbling of my brothers returning from their Vegas trip put me at ease a little bit, even though this broad had me standing here with more questions than answers.

She cringed and frowned as she caught sight of the crew, shrinking down low in her seat like she wanted to disappear.

"Aw, I see the two of you are finally reunited," Colt teased. "You like your surprise?" I shook my head and flicked him off. He was my best friend, the only friend I'd ever had in the world at one point in my life, and I had no idea where I'd be without him, but sometimes his decision-making skills were strange. "It was all Reena, by the way. I just saw it as an excuse to work on our kidnapping skills."

"What?" I stammered. "They kidnapped you?"

"I wouldn't give 'em that much credit," she said. "They had good timing."

"Now I'm wondering what the fuck you're doing sitting outside in the open here, missy. I thought you were supposed to be in hiding," Colt scolded. She pouted her lips and rolled her eyes.

"Mom was driving me nuts. She tried to put me in Rubin's old room."

"Aw, old Moses would probably enjoy the company. He just got fed last night, didn't he? He probably wanted to play."

Now she was flicking him off, and I was more confused than I was before. Who was she hiding from? What was that all about? I knew better than to ask right now. She'd

## Judas

tell me when she was good and ready, but it just added to my concern for her.

"Come on," I said. "You can have my room while we get this shit sorted out." I parked my bike and grabbed her by the arm. Her skin was softer than I remembered, but her body felt so delicate, like all her bones might break if I grabbed her the wrong way. "You need to eat and you need to sleep, then you need to tell us what the hell is going on."

I led her to my room, showed her around, and went and grabbed her a big plate of scrambled eggs, a pile of bacon, a stack of pancakes, and six pieces of peanut butter toast from the buffet Reena had laid out for the men's return. She was fresh out of the shower when I got back, her long blonde hair dripping all over the tile, her eyeliner a huge black smear, shocking against her pale skin. Her tattoos looked so bright up against that stark white towel, and I couldn't help but imagine myself tracing that big floral masterpiece that started on her upper chest and twisted down her ribs with my mouth. I already knew exactly where it went. I'd seen it on display every week since she got it, just not up close and personal like this.

I couldn't deny my attraction to her, and now, with her nearly naked body so close to me, it was even harder to deny the way my cock was straining up against my jeans. In person, she was so much better: the way she smelled, the way she moved, the way she reacted to the way I was staring at her.

"I'm sorry," I stammered. "I should give you some privacy." I turned my back to her, fishing through my dressers for a t-shirt and some shorts she could throw on. I didn't know what she had in her backpack. I turned to hand her the clothes, and her towel was gone, tossed on the floor. She stood in front of me, naked as the day she was born, and I struggled to pick my jaw up off the floor. "Here," I said, thrusting the clothes at her, turning my eyes to the ground.

"Don't act like you haven't seen it before," she said, reaching for my chin.

"That's different, Athena. That's a different you. That's your career. When you're under this roof, that's not you. That's not how I think about you. Now go put some clothes on and eat some food."

It was hard to deny her beauty, but I knew right now this wasn't a sex thing. This was her trying to work through her shit. Maybe she was trying to make me feel like shit.

"Then why did you watch? If you don't think about me that way, why did you watch?"

"I gotta go," I said. "Help yourself to whatever. I'll crash at Colt's tonight. Eat some food, get some sleep, figure out what the fuck you're doing here."

I didn't have the words to tell her I watched because it was the only way I could be certain she was alright. It was the only connection I had with a woman I felt more strongly about than anyone I'd ever met in my life. I couldn't help that she turned me on. That's how the woman you loved was supposed to make you feel. I watched because I needed to make sure she was healthy. I needed to pretend like she was happy. I needed a sign that she had officially moved on from this life. When that day came, I'd stop watching.

Now that she was back here in the house, standing naked in my room, I felt like a dog chasing a car tire. I didn't know what the fuck to do with her. She obviously didn't want to be here. She definitely didn't want me. She needed us, but I had no idea why.

I shut the door behind her and walked out into the clubhouse, trying to get my dick to cooperate, but I couldn't get that vision of her out of my mind. Not her tits or the little strip of white blonde hair that looked like an arrow heading straight to her pussy, or the idea that I finally had a chance to make her mine once and for all. The two of us all grown up, I could give her the life she always deserved. I'd make her a queen. It was going to be her choice, though, not my demand.

# 17

## Athena

How to confront your porn star career in front of real-life people you know 101:

Take off your clothes.

It'll either make them really fucking uncomfortable or you'll find out real fast exactly why they're being so nice to you. At least that's the way it's always worked with most men.

Not Judas, though. That strange bastard didn't even bat an eye. Of all the men in the world who I wouldn't be completely disgusted with if he made a move, he didn't even seem to notice. Now I was sitting here with a fist full of bacon, wrapped in a t-shirt that smelled like all things him, and I felt like, in this strange little standoff we were having, he had the upper hand.

Sure, I wanted him. How could any woman not? He had the body of a god, and that stoic darkness that he wore on his face, that strange peace with the life that he'd chosen that permeated the air around him, it was sexy as fuck. Electric. If I knew one thing about Judas, though, he always said what he meant, and something he said, I couldn't let drop.

*You left us when we needed you.*

He thought I was a selfish bitch, but for some reason he didn't hate me. Sure, he was being cold. Maybe I was, too. I often wondered what would happen if we ever saw each other again. It was going pretty much exactly as I imagined it.

I wrapped his comforter around my shoulders as I finished eating the giant breakfast laid before me. He obviously knew I was starving. I swear, between the half loaf of peanut butter toast and the pancake the size of my head, he was trying to put me in diabetic shock, but I ate every bite. The bacon made me laugh the most. I wondered if he had to put gloves on to touch it.

I hadn't felt this safe and content in a long time, and yet there was a sadness I couldn't shake. A sadness in knowing I couldn't just stay here in this moment forever. I had to move on. Then again, maybe nobody was looking for me. Maybe nobody noticed the missing money. The men I stole from were all extremely well off. 10K was just a drop in the bucket.

There was really only one way to find out. I was so wide awake exhausted, my body was trying to go to sleep, but my mind wouldn't let it drop. A simple google search could probably put my mind at ease, at least for a couple hours. Then, I could wake up, talk to the guys, and figure out my game plan. Hiding here was the best option for now, but it was a band-aid on a bigger problem. I had no idea who had seen me in the hours since I left Vegas, but the fact that the truck I was riding around in was wrapped in a giant sticker of the Indignant Few logo, and all the men with me were wearing cuts of the same pointed a giant blinking arrow right here to the clubhouse.

Maybe I could just live in denial and wait for my fate to catch up with me. The more I looked around this strange but familiar room, the more I thought about Judas, the easier it was for me to picture myself an old lady, his old lady. Maybe we could get a little farmhouse, I could pop out babies and pretend like I didn't know what he was doing when he didn't come home at night. I could let myself go, focus on trying to raise well-balanced kids in a life they'd never choose for themselves. If I could do a little better than my mama and daddy, that would be alright, right?

*Snap the fuck out of it, Athena. That's the kind of shit thinking that got your father and most of his men killed. Live in denial and somebody will definitely kill you when you have your dick out.*

I grabbed Judas's laptop, breathing a sigh of relief that it wasn't password protected. His background picture was of him and a shaggy mutt with three legs. They both looked like they were smiling ear to ear. I didn't think I'd ever seen him smile like that before. He was such an odd duck. His little off quirks were endearing in their own right, maddening on a level of trying to understand what was going on in his head, though.

I pulled up a browser, and as I went to search my name, all I had to type in was Ath and pages and pages of search history of my full name popped up. *Should I be flattered or creeped out?* I wondered what went through his mind when he saw what I was doing. I suddenly felt extremely naked. I'd never been ashamed at my history in porn; I'd always been extremely sex positive. It was always all in good fun. At least that's what I convinced myself. I wondered if he saw it that way too, or if he was secretly judging me this whole time? That's how most men were—dying to get me in bed, but disgusted to be seen with me in public.

## Judas

Judas wasn't like other men, though. Not even a little bit.

I was dying to check my email. Harold was probably going nuts by now. The only phone number he had of mine was the one for the phone I left behind, laying on my bed. I was positive after not showing up for my show last night, my fans were going equally crazy. It was obvious from the tweets that showed up on the first page of the search result, trending hashtag #wheresathena. Of course Harold was casually responding to all of them with comments like "she's recovering from a stomach bug, she sends her love to all of you XOXO", but my fans weren't dummies.

It was an insane concept to me. Fans. People who didn't even know me but loved me in ways that my family never even showed me. They were genuinely concerned about my well-being, not just because I put on a good show. Living right up in that lifestyle, it was easy to separate myself from them, pretending like they were just faceless keyboard warriors, but now that I was feeling more alone in the world than ever, I started feeling this twinge of compassion toward them.

Maybe I should log in to Twitter, just to give everybody some peace of mind. I began to type in my log-in details, then realized how fucking stupid I was being. I was letting my ego get in the way of my safety.

I scrolled down a little further.

"Bitch ran off with my money #wheresathena" a tweet from a man with the screen name bruno67 had written. It had fifty likes and twenty retweets. The hair on my arms stood up straight.

"Somebody deliver me that slut #deadoralive #wheresathena" another one read, this one from josephlee44. A hard lump formed in my throat as I gulped for air.

"You think this is a game? Hope you had your fun. We're coming for you. We have men all over the world looking for your sweet ass, and when they find you, all bets are off. We don't even need the money. It's the principal #wheresathena #1000000reward" from anonymousinvegas. I immediately slammed the screen shut, backing away from the computer as quickly as I could. My heart was racing. They were definitely coming for me. This was not a game.

I knew the men had limited awareness as to what was up, only knowing what Isaac told them about why we had to bail last night. I needed to show them this. My very presence here was compromising their lives as well as my own.

Telling them would probably mean more running, though. More running that I definitely wasn't ready to do right now. My body felt weak and tired, going on almost twenty-four hours without sleep, the last nap I took a Benadryl-induced coma thanks to my wasp stings. I needed to get my energy back. I needed a few hours to breathe. I double-checked the lock on the door. I took my pistol from my backpack and slid it under the pillow. I turned out the lights, the room pitch-black and silent. Just a few hours of rest and I could start back on my mission. I wasn't going to sleep too heavily; I'd hear anybody coming from a mile away.

I hugged his pillow tight to my body, something about it feeling oddly comforting. I wasn't supposed to feel safe here. That was how they sucked you in, but for one moment of delusional denial, I let myself think as long as I had Judas around, everything was going to be alright. I might be distanced from my family, but they'd never give up my cover. They'd never sell me out; at least that was my solitary prayer. It didn't take long before my brain caught up with my body and I was out like a light.

My dreams took me to a place where I had been longing to go for ages, only the Montana cowboy was now a tall, muscle-bound biker. It didn't matter where we were. As long as he was around, I was at home.

# 18

## Judas

"Coming in hot," Rosie shouted as he wheeled the massive carpet extractor off the ramp of the trailer. Our secretary, he was tall as a tree, dumb as a rock, and a favorite amongst the ladies. It was probably a sight to behold, our biker gang standing around geeking out over cleaning equipment, but anything that would make our job easier was a welcomed addition to the arsenal.

"Three hundred bucks," Breaker said. "These things retail for over four grand." He pulled his long brown hair back with a rubber band and started ripping the machine apart on the concrete floor of the garage. That kid was crazy like that, obsessed with what the inside of everything looked like. He was a great treasurer, though, and the auction was definitely worth the trip from the looks of the haul.

Miles jumped so high he damn near hit the ceiling as he flipped the switch on the industrial floor buffer and it started to rotate across the room with a loud whir. "That shit would've come in handy last night," he said.

Last night felt like a decade away.

## Judas

"Decker said y'all did a bang up job," Colt said. "Sorry I had to miss it." I rolled my eyes at him. He lived for any chance he got to get his hands dirty. I, on the other hand, preferred things a little more quiet around here. I handed him the envelope of cash.

"You guys are so cute," Tressica shouted from the garage door, "playing with your new toys." She was dressed in her work clothes, black high heels and a pencil skirt that was so tight it left nothing to the imagination. It still blew my mind such a hot smart chick was slumming it with us. Slumming it with my married best friend.

"I'll show you cute," Colt said, grabbing her around the waist, kissing her passionately on the lips until she turned a bright shade of red. He heaved her over his shoulder, his hand cupping her round ass, and wandered off. Nobody could deny that they were a perfect match. That broad turned Colt into a totally different man than his usual cocky asshole self. It was probably why he still kept Zelda around. He knew if he committed to Tress full-time he'd officially have to straighten up. I didn't know how much longer she was willing to put up with his shit, but as of this moment, they were like two teenagers in love.

"What about you?" Law asked, poking me in the ribs with his elbow. "I didn't think you'd be leaving your room for a solid week." Even when he teased, he looked angry, serious. That man had seen some shit. He'd worked for government agencies we didn't even know existed. Our enforcer, he was the smartest guy out of all of us; brains and brawn, a double threat. The only time I ever saw him smile was when he was trying to figure out complicated shit, digging bullets out of arteries, or hacking complicated computer systems.

"Y'all aren't right," I said. "What was the point of that?" I still hadn't figured out why they went to the effort to drag her back here if she didn't want to be here. I still didn't understand what the hell that had to do with me.

"We were sick of you moping around all the time. Plus Reena wouldn't stop bitching," Delaney said. "Dude, we delivered you your dream woman, who happens to be a porn star, and you're standing here with your hands in your pockets?"

"She's crazy about you, brother," Breaker said. "Law had her all drugged up and she wouldn't stop rambling about you on the ride to the hotel. Hours and hours of 'where's Judas' and 'I miss Judas.' Whatever you did to that bitch, she never forgot about you, that's for sure. I think you're the only reason why she even agreed to come back."

"You drugged her?" I asked, trying to control my temper. It was like everyone in the world was just trying to make me snap in the last twenty-four hours. "Y'all kidnapped her and drugged her?"

"She was having an allergic reaction to the wasps," Law explained. "Is her face still all swollen up? How about her ankle? She twisted it pretty good."

"What the fuck did you guys do to her?" I shouted.

"There it is," Delaney chuckled. "Reena totally called it. Our little Judas is in love."

"Fuck off," I said. I wasn't in love. Sure, I felt for her in ways that I didn't understand, but I knew one thing: I wasn't going to fight for some broad who didn't even want to be here. I wasn't going to put myself out there for somebody who was just going to run off again. I'd rather spend the rest of my life alone and miserable than waste it on chasing around some bitch who didn't care about me. She'd made it perfectly clear she hated the club. She made it perfectly clear that in her mind I was no different than any of the other dudes who jerked off to her porn videos. "She's taking a nap and then she's out of here."

"Absolutely not," Law said sternly. "She's tangled up in some bad shit. If she wants to keep on living, she's not going anywhere. Not right now at least. Not til we figure out how to get her out of this mess."

My mind went back to the conversation on the porch, Colt scolding her for her being outside. She was obviously in trouble. Law explained the situation, the cash cards she maxed out but swore it wasn't supposed to be like that, the kind of people she robbed. When he pulled out his Twitter and showed me what was trending in terms of her name, I felt the rage start burning inside me, stronger than I'd felt it in a long time.

She was in serious danger.

Lucky for her, she was in the right place. Maybe she didn't give a shit about me, but deep down, I knew she was the only women I'd ever truly love. I wasn't going to let anybody hurt her ever again, especially not these keyboard warriors and their threats, putting a bounty on her head like she was some sort of prized possession. I had half a mind to call them out. Call them here. Show them what the Indignant Few were capable of, and what happened when they fucked with one of our own.

She had to come around. I was going to show her a side of me that she never saw before, the side of me that made me the man everyone feared as much as respected. Whoever said 'this isn't a game' was right. I was done playing with her. *Athena Morgan Fisher, it's time you figured out who you really are.* I was going to show her, whether she liked it or not.

## 19

## Athena

I wasn't sure how long I passed out for. The nightstand lamp was flicked on, and a plate of food wrapped in tinfoil sat on the little island that separated his bedroom from the kitchen. I shivered from head to toe as I hopped out of bed. Judas had always liked things really cold. Clinical. Exactly like how he acted toward me earlier today.

There was a bright pink beach bag sitting on the armchair in the corner of the room with a yellow Post-it note stuck to the top. "Just to get you through until you have time to go shopping. Sorry if it's way too big, XO Tress," it read. I wondered how she got in without me hearing her. The thought sent a chill down my spine. I needed a better security system. Apparently I wasn't as light a sleeper as I thought.

My stomach was growling loudly, and I devoured the plate of fried chicken and macaroni salad that was left on the table. If there was one redeeming quality about my mama, it was that she knew her way around the kitchen. For all I knew, she laced it with poison, but at least I'd die a happy woman.

## Judas

I dumped the bag of clothes out on the bed. Tressica always had a great sense of style, and that definitely hadn't changed. Her taste was even better, a lot more expensive than it was when we were growing up. I couldn't believe some of the names on the tags. She might not be a lawyer, but whatever she was doing, she was raking in some major cash. I took the sheer maxi dress—long sleeved and ruffly, totally bohemian, black with yellow flowers—and held it up to my body. Something about the perfect dress was enough to bring a smile to my face. I might be a piece of shit petty criminal hiding out in a den of crazies, my life might be completely off the rail, but at least I could look pretty.

Tressica was a damn angel and none of us deserved her. Tucked in the bag was a basic makeup kit, a curling iron, and all the toiletries a girl could ask for. What such a thoughtful and put together woman wanted from my brother was beyond my comprehension.

I took my time getting ready, knowing nobody would really care whether I came out of this room wearing a burlap sack and a towel on my head or a prom gown, but something about making myself presentable made me feel like, for one instant, that I had my shit together, even though I knew everything was falling apart.

I needed to show the guys those tweets. I owed it to them to show them what they were getting themselves into by keeping me around. I swooped some dark blue eye shadow over my eyelids, wondering why I'd never tried this shade before. It had been my job all these years to look good, and less than a whole day back at the clubhouse and I was already learning things about my skin tone that I'd never even considered before.

This kind of thinking was hella toxic.

I was reverting to my old ways. Not even twenty-four

hours back at my old home, and here I was painting on my face and whistling a happy tune, in complete denial about the severity of my situation. I was turning into my mother. Maybe I had always been her, but being away from this place let me hide that side of myself better than before.

I'd always promised myself I wouldn't be some weak bystander, a pretty face, a damsel in distress, and yet here I was curling my hair and globbing on body glitter like some stupid bitch trying to catch a date.

I wasn't, though. At least I could try and tell myself that. Sure, my feelings for Judas were strong, but he was already accounted for. Not just by Betty Sue. He was accounted for by the club, the patch, the life I swore off. This was all just temporary.

Maybe I could just hide in here while I let things calm down a little. I could live in the darkness and pretend like I was sleeping every time someone came in to feed and water me. I hadn't had a vacation in years. Maybe if I decompressed for a while, I'd get my wits back. I'd be that no-holds-barred boss babe who had everything under control.

I sat on the edge of the bed and stared at the wall. How did this guy function without a TV set? His bookshelf was impressive. If it were any other guy, I'd think it was just for show. Judas, however, I was sure he devoured *The Things They Carried* and *The 48 Laws of Power*. He was a complicated fellow.

I couldn't contain my curiosity any longer. I at least had to go do a lap around the clubhouse and see how things had changed over the last ten years. Would it be just like the old days? Thick smoke, drunken idiots, fistfights, and club sluts lined up wall-to-wall, looking for somebody to make them an old lady, or was Isaac not simply talking out his ass? Had things really changed around here?

## Judas

I cracked the door open, peeking out into the hallway. I could hear the loud roar of heavy metal coming through the swinging doors that led to the bar. I could hear the loud cackle of my mother's laugh, the sound of pool balls breaking on the table, the muffled voices of the new generation of the MC. I thought I'd never want any parts of this again, that I was all grown out of this phase, but the reality was, this life was like a drug I forgot I was addicted to. I couldn't resist the urge to belly up to the bar and crack open a beer, drinking myself into oblivion and pretending like the world wasn't such a bad place.

It was in me. It was in my blood. You could take the girl out of the MC, but you couldn't take the MC out of the girl. I smoothed my dress and tossed my hair. It was time for Athena Fisher to make her first official appearance post-kidnapping.

## 20

## Judas

The clubhouse was pretty mellow tonight, even though the bitches were on their worst behavior after a weekend without the guys around to feed them attention then shit on their dreams. I always wondered what had to happen in a woman's life to make them that way, draw them to this life, a life that was fun until it wasn't. A life that turned you into a commodity. Sure, it was a fast track into our dysfunctional family, but at the end of the day, no matter how many brothers you slept with, you were still alone. It was a different kind of love than the outside world understood, maybe a mutual appreciation, but to me, it didn't feel good.

I took a pull from my pipe, letting the smoke sort of lull me into a state of simply existing. I was present as much as this barstool underneath me was. Here but not really thought about. Functional if called upon, but not going out of my way to participate. I didn't have much to say anyway.

Nobody here understood what was going on in my mind anyway. They thought bringing Athena back here was a joke. They thought they were doing me a favor, like hiring a stripper for a bachelor party or something. They didn't understand why the two of us didn't just hump and get it over with.

I was too worried about the girl in my room, not just because of the people who were after her. She was my holy grail. The woman I waited my whole life for. I could protect her from the outside world, but could I protect her from myself?

I watched her sleep today, her pretty face the only thing peeking out from underneath the pile of blankets. I didn't try to wake her, but I didn't try not to either, turning the light on, talking to Tressica as she dropped off the bag of clothes, trying to go about my business as usual. Every time I looked over at her, I got this weird feeling in my guts. She was smiling so sweetly, looking so content and comfortable. Knowing she could feel like that around me, even when she was at her most vulnerable, unconscious to the world, it messed with my head. It took everything in me not to just spoon up next to her, finally wrap my body around hers after all these years, squeeze her until she knew this was exactly where she was supposed to be. Forever.

Except I knew that wasn't true. She belonged here about as much as that alligator did. Sure, we could keep him happy and fed, but he knew as much as we did this wasn't where he really belonged. He'd run away the first chance he got and rip us all to shreds on his way out the door.

Just like she would.

Just like she did.

The front door swung open with a squeal and it would've been funny the way everyone turned to look, everyone reaching for their pistols without thinking, but the fact that it was because we were potentially under attack, that any minute now the guys looking for Athena could come busting through that door looking to make this a real bad night, made it a little less laughable.

To everyone's dismay, it was only Isaac. I'm sure a couple of the guys probably wished they could shoot him. Hell, there were days I definitely wanted to. He didn't belong here. He would never be like us. I figured by now he would've worked his way out. It was the only reason I got Colt to agree to let him prospect. The man never liked to get his hands dirty unless he was shitting on someone else to get ahead, and he'd been handling dumpster duty and cleaning up after rallies like a boss. Every time I thought he'd changed for the better, though, he'd start with his abrasive bullshit. It sucked being personally responsible for him after all these years, but as fucked-up as what he did to me was, I would've never been where I am today without him.

"Where's the broad?" was the first thing that came out of his mouth as he slid up beside me, motioning to Elaine for a beer.

"What's it matter to you?" I asked. He might've broken Betty Sue down, but that was the kind of bitch she was. Athena was the kind of girl who could see right through his bullshit. "You got no business with prez's sister anyway. You stay in the prospect pool."

He chuckled in a way that reminded me of my cousin Bert. It was chilling. We might be twins, but that kinda sound never came out of my mouth. It was needlessly sadistic, like an old-school villain who just tied somebody to the train tracks. Not Indignant material at all. I wished he wasn't my blood brother so I could send him out to pasture for that idiotic laugh alone.

"You misread me, Jude," he said. He blew the buxom bartender a kiss and dangled a five-dollar bill in front of

## Judas

him before stuffing it down her tight leather halter top. She made a gagging sound before quickly wandering off. He even crept the bitches out, and those girls were into some nasty shit.

"The fuck is that?" I asked, swiveling in my stool so we were face-to-face. Hanging from his wrist was my gold watch. My grandpa's watch.

The only thing I could think of when I looked at his grinning face was how his teeth were way too straight. They needed realigned. I clenched my fist in my lap.

"What?" he asked, still smiling like a goon.

"You know exactly what." I stood up from my barstool. So much for a chill night. It was one thing for him to fuck with Betty Sue. It was another thing for him to keep rubbing it in my face every chance he got. I personally gave zero fucks about what he did with her. What I did take issue with was the fact that he was going out of his way to try and get me to snap. I saw it from a mile away. He was a one-trick pony. Predictable as he'd ever been.

"I got it back for you, buddy," he said, sliding it from his wrist and holding it out for me. "That bitch was going to pawn it." I relaxed my fists and sneered at him. "I know how much it means to you. Hell, I wish we had more than just a couple hunks of metal to remember Mom and Dad by."

I snatched it from his hand, sliding it into my back pocket. "Grow the fuck up, man," I said. "Why do you always have to be so sleazy? Why can't you just act like a normal person?" Looking around the room, it was obvious what I was saying was ridiculous. Sure, we had our own scale of normal people. Colt was snuggled up on a sofa with his 'girlfriend', Rosie was giving himself a crooked-ass shamrock tattoo on his upper thigh with a homemade gun that looked dirtier than anything I'd ever seen in prison while Miles watched in horror, and Breaker was barely poking out from underneath a pile of writhing half-dressed bitches as usual.

The difference between us and him?

He was just cruel. We were just *us*. He'd never be us. I wished he'd just tap out already.

Suddenly, a strange quiet washed over the room. Even the music seemed muted.

Athena was making her first appearance out of the darkness after arriving here this morning. That woman could turn heads in a pair of sweatpants and an oversized t-shirt, but the dress she was wearing, this see-through flowing thing covered in flowers, was enough to make my heart lodge itself in my throat. She looked like a model. A goddess. Her ruby red lips were plump, even though her smile was thin. She looked around curiously, like she was wandering into the clubhouse she grew up in for the first time, not making eye contact with anybody, but instead running her fingers over the wood on the wall, the barstools.

Nobody said a word. She had to have known every eye in the room was on her. I was trying not to stare but I couldn't help myself. I fought my urge to claim her right here, grab her around the waist and tell everyone in the room to fuck off, to stop looking at her, she was mine and always had been.

I was too late.

Isaac walked over to her, his chest puffed out, and wrapped his arms around her. I could tell from the look in her eyes over her shoulder that she was overwhelmed. I started over to them, fully planning on taking him to the ground once and for all, for the first time in a long time walking that dangerous ledge when, out of nowhere, she started cracking up.

She relaxed, cupping his chin in her hand, not in a tender way, but in a mama bear kind of way, and shook her head. "Don't sneak up on women like that, ya creep," she said. "You're bound to get yourself decked."

"Wouldn't be the first time," he said with a shrug.

"I'm sure. You need to start taking lessons from these scumbags," she laughed. "If they're anything like their forefathers, bitches line up down the block to take a ride on their 'bikes.' "

"Awe, 'Thena, you're not a bitch," he said. I could've swore he looked over his shoulder and winked right at me. "You're a princess, and I want to be the first one who gets to buy you a beer."

"Flattery will get you nowhere, son. I drink for free anyway." She turned and walked straight toward me, and I was weak in my knees. She was still the same girl I knew all those years ago, only somehow a million times hotter. I couldn't even look her in the eye; the only thing I could focus on was the fact that she wasn't wearing any shoes, her tiny feet dragging on the filthy floor of the bar. It was sexy in a strange way, a carefree 'this is my home and I don't give a fuck' kind of way.

Only my dumbass would read into a woman without any shoes on. I guess it was just wishful thinking. I wanted her the same as she always was, only different. I wanted her to be the kind of woman who stays.

"Say who you drink free, sis?" Colt asked, stepping in between the two of us. "You got more than enough dirty money to buy this place ten times over."

"You never earned a clean dollar in your life, you dumpster diver. The only thing clean about you is your laundry, and that's because Mom still washes it. Unless she still bathes you, too. I wouldn't be surprised."

"That's what I got Tressica for," he said. "She gives the

best baths. She's very thorough if you know what I'm saying." He flicked his tongue at her and she slapped her hands over her eyes. "Nobody drinks for free unless they got a patch on."

"I'm legacy," she said, holding her ground, motioning for Elaine.

"You're nothing but a damn traitor." He put his hand up in the air, and Elaine stopped in her tracks. She looked confused. President's say trumped everything. Under normal circumstances, that is.

"You brought me here, ya fucking idiot," she said with a laugh. "What would Dad say?"

"I don't know. Why don't you go dig him up and ask him?"

"Mom!" she shouted. Reena just lifted her head up off the bar and waved her hand at them. I was having déjà vu. Things were no different now than they were twenty years ago.

"If you're not good, we'll just call up anonymousinvegas and hand you over," Colt said. "I could probably show him a thing or two about how to torture you."

"Colt," I shouted, "that's not fucking funny."

"Yeah," Tressica said, pushing herself between the two of them. "Quit being a dick. As long as she's under this roof, nobody's gonna fuck with her. Including you, you immature asshole." He shoved his hands in his pockets and walked away. I didn't know what it was about her, but she seemed to have a way with him. Any other woman talked to Colt like that and she'd be dumped in the woods somewhere trying to find her way back to town with nothing but the flashlight on her cell phone. "Somebody get this girl a beer, please. Put it on my tab."

Elaine stood there motionless except for the nervous

flutter of her long black eyelashes. "You don't have a tab," she nervously peeped.

"She doesn't have a tab, Colt! And she doesn't have a patch? Somebody call the party police," Athena roared, chasing after her brother. He scooped her up in his arms and hugged her, and Elaine lined up shots on the bar for everyone. At least one sibling rivalry around here was purely for show.

"Welcome to the club," Tressica said, holding up her shot glass to mine as I watched Colt and Athena fake wrestle, her legs swinging wildly as her dress wrinkled up over her hips. "You probably know better than I do that these two are a whole lot of nonsense."

"I don't think I'm a part of that club, babe," I said, taking down the shot of whiskey, grimacing at the afterburn. Hell, my brother had spent more time with her than I had since she got back.

"Oh, you totally are. You just don't know it yet." She tipped back her beer and smiled contentedly at the duo.

I couldn't help but smile, too. It felt like something that had been missing in my life for a long time had been locked back into place. The mood of the house as a whole felt lighter.

"I love this song!" Athena squealed, as an old Kid Rock song blasted from the speakers. "Tress, dance with me!" Tressica balanced two shot glasses on the palm of her hand and picked up two bottles of beer in the other, and the two started dancing like no one was watching. I was trying not to, at least, but it was hard seeing her perfect body gyrating on Tressica. Definitely made my jeans feel a little tighter, especially because I knew exactly what was underneath that sheer dress.

She took right back to the club life like a fish to water, and the rest of the room came to life. Everyone was dancing, laughing, and taking shot after shot. Isaac was right about one thing; she was a princess.

And she was totally eye fucking me from over Tress's shoulder. I turned away, thinking maybe I'd been staring at her unwittingly and she was trying to make me uncomfortable, but as I looked back over, she gestured to me. That perfect blonde with the hair that hung down to her ass, the girl I always had a little crush on who was now a full-grown woman, she was motioning me to come dance with her.

She knew damn straight I wasn't a dancer.

This was all a part of her game. My desire to put my body all over hers trumped my desire to look cool in front of my friends. I beelined my way to her, and she took my hand and pressed it to her hip, swaying back and forth to the beat of the music.

"You know the last time I danced was at your brother's wedding?" I leaned down and whispered in her ear, my mouth just inches from her flesh. God, she smelled like heaven, a little bead of sweat trickling down her neck.

"You know supposedly the whole reason why I was brought here was because of you?" she snapped back. "Don't deny it."

I spun her around and held her close, our faces nearly touching. "That's what I'm told," I said with a wink. "I don't think either one of us had much say in it."

"Why do you still give a damn about me after all these years?" she asked. "Why are you the only person who cares?"

"Am I not good enough?"

"Don't be ridiculous," she said, her lips turning into a pout. "If anything, it's the opposite." I just laughed and hung my head, happy to finally be near her, happy that whatever pent-up anger she had toward me was just probably from her lack of sleep. I pulled her tighter, letting her feel exactly what effect her grinding was having on me. She bit her lip and moaned a little. I'd never heard that moan from her before, and Lord knows I'd heard a lot in all my years of cyberstalking her.

"I think your phone's ringing," she whispered in a voice that was equal parts sexy and amused.

"Fuck it," I said as my phone vibrated in my pocket. "Everything I care about is in this room." She looked at me like I was kidding, but I wasn't. My crew. My family. The woman of my dreams. My motorcycle was parked safely in the garage; I'd buy another one if it meant I got to spend another minute tangled up with this wild beauty, and that's about the most intense compliment I could think of. I didn't need to tell her though.

I probably looked like a damn fool, stepping all over both of our feet as we danced a couple songs. My phone wouldn't quit, though.

"I appreciate the vibration. It's very thoughtful," she said, "but if you're not going to answer it, I will." She reached her hand in the wrong pocket, grazing my stiff cock as she giggled. "Oops."

"You better be careful," I said. "That thing hasn't felt a hand other than my own in a pretty long time. It's probably liable to explode if you rub it the wrong way."

"What's a pretty long time?" she asked. "A day? A week?" I shook my head. "A month?"

I didn't know the exact day it was, but it was shortly after Betty Sue and I broke up, and I tried to get my rebound on with as many club sluts as I could handle. It was an oddly unsatisfying phase, and it was probably close to a year ago.

"Oh my god, you're like a virgin all over again," she teased, dropping her jaw dramatically. "I don't know how I feel about stealing your innocence."

"You're still gonna do it anyway, right?" I asked, raising my eyebrow. She wasn't stealing anything from me except my heart. She might have porn star experience, but I knew my way around. I might even have a trick or two up my sleeve she'd never experienced before.

"Oh definitely. That phone is going to drive me fucking nuts, though. Will you get it?"

I didn't recognize the number when I pulled my phone out of my pocket. I handed it to her, not even thinking twice. I had nothing to hide from her.

"Hello?" she asked into the phone. A few seconds passed and she rolled her eyes and covered the receiver. "This is gonna be fun," she said to me with a wink.

## 21

## Athena

I knew enough about Betty Sue just by the things Isaac had told me and the way she acted when I met her earlier that this bitch had to go. She wasn't going to play cock-block, and she sure as hell had no right to be leeching off Judas anymore. Why nobody had stepped in sooner was beyond me. It was like I was back here for a reason, not just because I was hiding out, not just because my brother dragged me here. My people needed me. The club needed me.

This man I loved needed me. *Holy fuck. I'd have to get back to that thought later.*

Right now, I needed to shut this shit show down.

"What are you trying to pull, bitch?" I asked. She was wailing into the phone like a crazy person, not making any coherent sort of sentences. "You need to stop calling. It's time for you to leave my man alone." *That was an intense choice of words.* I could always say I was joking, or I was just doing what needed to be done. I kind of had a feeling I meant it though. He looked about as confused as I did at my outburst.

"Help!" she screamed. "Please, I just need help."

"Damn right you do. Maybe you should be calling Jesus instead, Betty Sue."

The way she was sobbing was over the top, bordering hysterical. She sounded like she was out of breath. Who goes running at midnight?

"I'm serious," she said. "I think someone drugged me." I wanted to just brush her off; she was, after all, a huge fan of drugs, and very well may have drugged herself, but the way she was crying, she sounded like a genuine woman in distress. I might be a coldhearted bitch, but I couldn't just let someone suffer. I wouldn't be able to sleep tonight if I knew she was in danger. "I need someone to come get me."

"Where are you?" I asked. Of all the damn things in the world I wanted to be doing right now, taking care of Judas's ex was nowhere on that list. Nobody in this room was sober enough to be driving around picking up skanks. We already had more than enough here in my opinion anyway. At the very least, I could call her a cab though. They could take her right back to whatever crazy farm she escaped from.

"Isaac," she kept shouting. "Isaac."

"No, you called the wrong twin, you sicko," I said. "What do you want me to do?" I asked Judas. "Your psycho ex keeps asking for Isaac." As if I said Bloody Mary into the mirror too many times, he appeared right next to me. He grabbed the phone out of my hand and promptly hung up.

"I'll go take care of it," he said. "I only had a couple of beers. Crazy bitch hopped in my truck earlier today. She was on some bad shit. I took her to my place to sleep it off. I didn't know what else to do. Didn't think you needed her running around here."

## Judas

I was thoroughly confused. Was she really that high all the time that she could mistake this skinny dweeb for his hunky twin? Was there more to this story than I was aware? The look on Judas's face was stone-cold. He didn't say anything, just snatched his phone back from his brother and turned and walked to the bar.

"It's complicated," Isaac said to me. "I'm just looking out for him." I never knew what to believe coming out of this guy's mouth, but I wasn't trying to let this situation take up more space in my head than it already was.

He walked out the door and nobody really gave him a second thought. I had a strange feeling 'it's complicated' was an understatement. There had to be a reason why they kept this guy around; I just really couldn't put my finger on it.

I followed Judas to the bar. He sat with a full bottle of beer in front of him, slowly peeling off the label.

"Frustrated?" I asked, offering him a thin smile.

"I'm sorry, Athena," he said. "This shit isn't none of your concern."

"Oh it is," I said, grabbing the bottle from his hand and pressing it to my lips. "Y'all brought me here? It's all my concern now."

## 22

## Athena

I took his hand in mine, squeezing it. Everything was starting to make perfect sense. For the first time in a long time, I felt needed. I felt like I was exactly where I was supposed to be. My fans, they might have enjoyed my body, got pleasure from the things I did on camera, and hell, they might have even felt a connection to me, but being back at home was real. My love for him was real. My heart was in this club. This was where I belonged, even if it meant sleeping with one eye open and facing down the demons I left behind.

They needed me as much as I needed them.

"I'm sorry I said all that stuff. I didn't cause a problem, did I?" I didn't care if I did, but burning bridges was my style. He took people in his life more seriously. Relationships more seriously. I'm sure it had something to do with his parents and that factory shooting all those years ago. He didn't do well with people leaving.

"We've been done for over a year," he said. "You're probably gonna think I'm nuts, but I just don't know how to get her away from me. I don't touch her. I'm not nice to her. Only thing I do is pay her bills while she tries to get back on her feet. I feel like I'm responsible for her somehow."

"You do what?" I stammered. No wonder the bitch wouldn't leave. She had a free ride.

He shrugged his shoulders. "It's just what men do. She's got issues."

"We all have issues. She has a free meal ticket and no responsibilities. That doesn't sound like issues to me. You still love her?" I couldn't rightly think of any reason why in my mind that he would keep doing that for someone unless he still loved her. Maybe I was overstepping.

"I don't think I ever did," he said. "Guess I just didn't want to bail on her. I just want to be a good person, Athena."

I remembered clearly the day we picked him up from juvenile detention. The way he looked right now, hunched up, distant, like he was wearing the guilt of the world, it reminded me so much of that day. "You are a good person. You've always been a good person. That's why you're a magnet for bad. People know they can walk all over you. She's gotta go. Isaac, too. Those two are playing you like a fool."

"He's my brother, Athena. He's my blood."

"These men are your brothers," I said, pointing around the room. "These men would die for you. They'd kill for you. They might fuck with your ex, but only because they're assholes, not because they're trying to hurt you."

"You sound like your mother," he said.

"Worst pick up line ever, dude." Yet, I knew exactly what I was saying. I wore it well. I'd heard the pep talk many times before. Never thought I was going to have to use it. Never thought I'd be back here repeating history, but I knew it was right where I belonged.

He raised his eyebrow and shot me a sideways smile. He was attractive all the time, but when he smiled at me, I probably would've been inclined to take off my panties and hand them to him if I was wearing any. Seeing him happy was like being a part of a secret club, being a part of some inside joke. I wondered if I had what it took to experience that every day. I knew I would fight like hell to make it happen if he gave me the chance.

"I don't do pick up lines." He reached for my barstool, and pulled it closer to his effortlessly, his corded biceps rippling as I whooped in shock. He put his hand on my thigh, the warmth of his touch burning through the flimsy fabric of my dress. "You know how crazy you're making me?"

"I like crazy," I purred. "You know that."

He cracked his neck and licked his lips. His grip grew tighter, his hand moving up my thigh, closer and closer to the point of no return. I wasn't chickening out if he wasn't.

That look he was giving me was almost scary, like the calm before a storm that I was grossly underprepared for. The hairs on my arm stood up. I placed my hand on top of his, giving him the nod. I was ready to go right now. Everyone in the room was irrelevant. I couldn't even hear the music over the pounding of my heart in my ears. "You want to go?" he asked.

I couldn't get up from my stool fast enough, damn near taking out the entire row, nearly tripping over my feet as he grabbed my arm to steady me. So much for a stealthy exit. I couldn't care less what any of these clowns had to say, though. This was how it was going to be now.

His hand cupped my ass as we walked down the hallway, his firm possessive touch enough to bring a moan to his lip. Judas' touch was unlike any other one I'd felt, men

## Judas

or women's. Judas' touch was real. It wasn't just fun and games.

Nothing about this situation was fun and games, even though I was certain that whatever happened behind that bedroom door was going to probably be the most fun I've had in a long time.

Every second felt like hours as he fumbled with the key, and when the door finally swung open, I couldn't control myself. I grabbed his face, pressing his lips to mine for the first time ever. I moaned, feeling his tongue hungrily making its way into my mouth as his hands traveled up the back of my thighs, pulling my dress up with them. I couldn't remember if I'd ever been kissed like this before in my life. I couldn't remember anything before this kiss, though, his touch, his passion, his hunger for me literally leaving me breathless. This was what a kiss was supposed to feel like. Like the universe aligned just for the two of us. My legs were growing weak, my knees about to give out. I was overwhelmed, blushing, pressing my hips into his, and we hadn't even made it to second base.

I'd thought about this day, fantasized about him many times before, tried to picture exactly how it would've went down, if it'd ever went down, but that was all a distant fantasy. A never going to happen kind of scenario. I had no idea what I did to deserve my dreams coming true, I sure as hell hadn't been a good girl.

As I pulled his shirt up over his head, I quivered at the sight of his tattooed torso, chiseled pecs, abs hard and rippling under the touch of my hand. There was more to him than a perfect body, something about him so different than the kinds of bodies I'd been with, the fabricated type. He wasn't the kind of man who's only responsibility was to work out and look good for a camera.

He was 100% real man. That thick layer of chest

hair I raked my fingers through, the scar on his collarbone from who knows what sort of dirty work he did, every minor imperfection on his skin only added to his sexiness. He wasn't caked in make-up or orange with spray tan. Judas had a biker tan, the kind that came from riding around in the sun in a t-shirt. So real. So gorgeous.

His callused hands, traveling up my spine, unclasping my bra as my tits sprang free.

"These are nice," he said, holding them in his hands like he was comparing a set of cantaloups. I gasped at his touch, his grip firm as he circled my nipples with this thumbs.

"You hate em?" I asked, looking him in the eye, suddenly self conscious.

He shook his head, and tenderly pressed his lip to my nipple. "There's only one thing I hate about you, Athena, and it's more my problem than yours." He moved his lips to my other nipple, circling with his tongue until I nearly collapsed in his grip. He had a wide smile on his face, squeezing my breasts tighter and tighter. "It's the knowing that the harder I squeeze you, the faster you're going to slip through my fingers."

He let go of my breasts, and I stepped back, my body ready to go, but my heart feeling like he just drove a stake through it.

"I know this is fun and games to you, Athena, but this is my fucking life. I can't just chop off my hair and put on a pair of sunglasses and move across the country."

"Judas," I said, stroking the stubble of his beard with the back of my hand. I was holding back a tear. Nobody had ever cared about me this much before. I felt it in his presence, read it all over his face. "I'm here now. I'm not going away. Can't you just live for the moment?"

## Judas

"With you? No," he said. He picked his shirt up off the ground. "This was a bad idea."

"What the fuck?" I shouted, charging after him as he walked to the door. "I thought this wasn't a game, Judas. You can't just play with my mind and fucking leave."

"I'm just being a good man," he said. "I'll crash somewhere else until you figure out what you're going to do. Help yourself to whatever."

I grabbed him by the arm, harder than I intended to, my rage overcoming me, my need for him to stay, stay here and either fight with me or fuck me, I didn't care at this point.

"What'd you learn from, your dad?" he asked. He jerked his wrist from my grip, and I stared at him in shock. He cupped my chin in his hand, watching the tears flow from my eyes. "You're not going to come up here and make a mess of my life, Athena. Stop fucking with my head."

"You think you're being a good man?" I asked. "You people are the reason why I'm the way I am. You want me to stay here? Give me one good reason." He stared back at me, his eyebrow twitching. I could almost see his mind turning over a million clicks per second as he licked his lips.

He pushed me onto the bed with a swiftness that alarmed me and began to unbuckle his belt. I reached for his zipper, but he grabbed my wrists in his hand, pinning them over my head. "There is no reasoning with you, Athena," he said. "I learned that a long time ago." He pulled my panties off to the side, sliding a finger into my wetness as I trembled, pinned to the bed by his tight grip. "It doesn't matter what you say or do, you always get your own way, don't you?"

My lips turned up into a smile. I raised my eyebrow. I

nodded, easing my thighs open wider as he tugged down my panties and tossed them off to the side. The way he was looking at me like I held the secrets of the world between my legs, staring at me only in my eyes as he took off his jeans. I bit my lip and stared at the rock hard cock pointing at me, oozing with precum as he pumped it in his hand.

"No," he said, grabbing my chin in his hand once again. "You want me to give you a reason to stay? We're doing it on my terms. Now look me in the eye." My eyelids fluttered, my heart racing. He was intense in the way that he knew exactly how to grab me, not hard enough to hurt me, but just enough to let me know who was in charge. There was something so intimate about the way his bright blue eyes burned through mine as his hand explored my slit, thumb circling my clit, the weight of his cock resting on my thigh. My back arched into the mattress and I felt my eyes roll back in my head.

"Fine," he said, releasing his grip on me as I snapped to attention.

"You're mean," I whined.

"I want you here with me," he said.

"I've always been here with you," I whispered, a lump rising in my throat. "Every time I closed my eyes, no matter where I was. You've always been on my mind, Judas. I never left you. I just left."

He looked stunned, and I was stunned too at how easily the words fell out of my mouth. Every one of them were true, though. I'd never wanted anyone more than him. I just didn't want the bag of shit that came along with him. In my mind, there was never any man who could measure up to him.

"No more games," I said. I knelt on my hands and knees on the bed and softly took the tip of his erection in my fingers, feeling its velvety head, all the while staring up at him. He groaned and shuddered, and I shook my head and clicked my tongue. "See?" I teased. "It's not as easy as you think it is. When somebody rubs you just the right way…" I stuck out my tongue and traced it around the tip of his dick, my eyes locked on his. I took his girth in my mouth, wildly, lust burning through my body, using my tongue to beg him to stay here with me, even just for the night in the best way I knew how.

He was not apprehensive, nor was he gentle, and as he wrapped his hand around my hair and used the ponytail he made to work my head back and forth on his cock, I relaxed my jaw, gagging a little, eager to take him all in, watching his face the entire time.

"I've wanted you so long," he growled, "wanted to see those perfect lips wrapped around my cock." I moaned into him as he traced his hands down my back, cupped my ass in his hands, parted my folds once again and teased his thumb into my wet pussy. "I want it all Athena. I want you here," he said, sliding another finger into me, making me gasp.

He dragged my wetness from my pussy, sliding it up my slit until he circled my tightest hole. As he began to tease his finger into my ass, I screamed like a crazed woman, the fullness sending waves of pleasure through my body from my head to my toe. I could barely concentrate on the task at hand, instead just letting him take over. "I want you here, too," he said.

No cameras. No scripts. No bright lights in my face. Nobody calling the shots but this perfect man. Judas, my salvation. My rock. The way he was strumming at my clit while he worked his fingers in and out of me made my toes curl and my body shudder. I was so close. So fucking close.

And he knew it.

"That's it babe," he groaned, "I want you to come with my dick in your mouth. You want a reason to stay? It's because you're mine and you know it." I collapsed in the biggest orgasm I'd ever had in my life, gasping for air around his cock, but he was relentless.

He turned me over on my back, parting my legs and stroking my spit all over his dick, his eyes wild and his body coated in a thin layer of sweat, accentuating every last one of his perfectly carved muscles. He reached into his nightstand and pulled out a condom, and I laid there quivering, a huge smile across my face as I anticipated what was still to come. The way he gripped my hips and pulled me to the edge of the bed, one swift movement, it was the hottest thing I could imagine. He was a man who knew what he wanted.

Our eyes locked once again, and he started to slide his dick into my drenched hole, inch by inch, stretching me around his girth, gripping me by the hips hard enough to leave a spattering of fingerprints. Marking me. Taking me. Showing me I was his. I hooked my heels around his perfectly round ass, grinding into him as he thrusted in and out, my walls gripping him like I wanted to keep him there forever, my body trying to milk him for everything he had. All my fantasies were coming to life, and as I tilted my head back and began to climax again, I felt the familiar twitch of his cock. He grunted, his sweat dripping down onto me, and sunk his teeth into my shoulder as he began to cum. I dug my fingernails into his back. If he wanted to play for keeps, all these bitches needed to know he was mine, too.

He pressed his lips to mine, and we kissed passionately, slowly, as I felt him soften inside me. I could feel his heart pounding into my chest. I didn't know what was coming over me, but I burst into tears.

## Judas

"Thena?" he asked, stroking my hair from my face. He looked down at me with concern, slowly pulling out of me. He stood in front of me, silent.

I laughed through my tears, my face turning bright red with embarrassment. Something about this man brought out the softness in me. I didn't want to admit what was on my mind. I didn't want to admit that he had given me a perfectly good reason to stay. It wasn't because the sex was so good, so right, better than anything I'd ever had before.

It wasn't because I knew the club needed me, or that he needed me, or that I was hiding out from some men who wanted me dead.

It was because I loved him.

I loved him more than I'd ever loved anyone in my life, more than I loved myself. I just didn't know if I was strong enough to see past the patch and the lifestyle that came along with it. But maybe I could try.

"I'm sorry," I muttered. "That was just really impressive." I wiped the tears from my face and sat up, watching his perfect form as he walked to the bathroom to dispose of our evidence. He grabbed a couple bottles of water from the fridge and handed me a towel as he sat down on the bed next to me.

"What now?" he asked. "You want me to go?"

"Judas!" I said, wrapping my arm around him. "Are you sure you're an Indignant? You're supposed to kick me out. This is your room, ya know?"

"Athena, when I'm with you, I'm not an Indignant. When I'm with you, nothing matters but what we have. You understand that? I know you've been burned by the club. I know you've seen some shit your dad and the old heads used to do. That's not me."

He interlaced his fingers with mine. I'd known it this whole time.

"I'm not gonna beg you," he said, "but I will do whatever I can to show you. This club is my family, but you'll always have my loyalty. Having you here is the best and worst thing that's ever happened to me, girl. Knowing you might be gone tomorrow, it makes it hard to even look at you, and Lord knows all I want to do is stare at your perfect body all night long."

I rested my head on his shoulder. In this moment I wanted nothing more than to profess my love for him. I wanted to promise him I'd stay forever, that I'd make it work. I knew he would never do anything to hurt me purposely, but that wasn't what I was worried about.

Just as much as he feared losing me, I knew the day would come that I would have to lose him. That's the way this always worked. This club made widows. Was that a fate I was just willing to wait around for ignorantly?

*Live in the moment, Athena.*

Tonight was not the time for making any decisions. Tonight was the time for me and him to get under the covers and play dumb, drift off to sleep and pretend like this could be our future, our happily ever after. In the morning, I could face the future, with or without him. Right now, I just wanted to be near him, to make up for all of our lost years.

# 23

## Judas

Of course I woke up alone.

Maybe last night was just a dream. Maybe it was my worst nightmare coming into fruition. Athena'd left me once before. Having her for the first time was the worst kind of torture I could've imagined. I'd rather let Rosey waterboard me for six hours than play this sadistic mental game of maybe I will, maybe I won't get to spend the rest of my life with the woman I love.

My back was sore, my mouth dry, and I needed a hot shower and cup of coffee before I could even think about what I needed to get into today. Her stuff was still scattered all over my room, a weird change from the way I normally kept it. I'd be more than happy to live with her chaos if I knew it was a sign she was sticking around. I knew it wasn't, though. Last time she left here, she didn't even take a bag, just hopped in a car and stopped answering her phone.

This time was different though. She wasn't safe. There were men out to get her. I should've slept in front of the door. Even if she didn't want me, she didn't need to be out in the wild.

The door creaked open, and there she stood. Her jean shorts were so short and frayed, the pockets hung out of the bottom and they looked like they were going to fall down off her tiny frame. Her tits poured out over her polka dotted tank top. Her hair was up in a sloppy ponytail and she had on a full face of make-up.

"Don't look so happy to see me," she said, her voice dripping with sarcasm.

"Where'd you go?" I asked.

"I went to the gym with Tress. I brought you breakfast," she said, holding out a plate. "Mama said this is what you like."

"You don't need to be going to the gym," I said. I instantly regretted it when it came out of my mouth, knowing she'd probably take it the wrong way. She was basically a toothpick with tits these days, but I still thought she was sexy as hell. What I really meant was that she didn't need to be going anywhere.

She rolled her eyes at me. "Best cure for a hangover," she said. "I needed to sweat that shit out." She handed me the plate, but I didn't take it. Reality was hitting me about last night. To me it was everything. To her, I was probably just a stupid drunken mistake. As if she could read my face like a book, she took my hand and pressed it to her lips. "I didn't mean it that way. I just don't really drink anymore. I can't keep up with you guys."

Her freshly washed hair smelled so good. She unwrapped the foil covered plate, steam rolling off the breakfast burrito and baked sweet potato.

"This blows my mind," she giggled. "Most of ya'll are human garbage disposals. I watched Colt wrestle a piece of bacon off Miles' dog this morning after it fell on the floor."

## Judas

"Jesus, what time is it?" I asked. Maybe I'd drank a little too much last night too. We were supposed to start demoing the Anderson warehouse this week so we could turn it into a new 'storage facility.' It was a great location, out in the woods just far enough that nobody could hear you scream, and close enough to a bunch of major highways for transport purposes. Sat on a huge chunk of land, too.

"Relax," she said. "I moved some things around. I hope you don't mind, but you're stuck with me all day." She plopped down on the edge of the bed, and I couldn't help but stare at those long tanned legs. I'd rather have her for breakfast than this plate of food, but I appreciated her and her mom looking after me, so I stood there and ate while she watched intently.

"I think I'm going to turn myself in to the police," she said, pressing her finger to her lips. I nearly choked on my burrito.

"What?" I stammered. "Please tell me you're kidding."

"You want me to stay here? I want to do it the right way. I don't want to spend my life in hiding, Judas. I want to be with you, don't get me wrong, but I can't just be an old lady. I worked my ass off since I was seventeen. I built a career. I built a brand."

"You want to keep doing porn?" I asked. The thought really never crossed my mind. I had tolerated before, but before I had no choice. No old lady of mine was going to be fucking dudes for money, that was for certain. I could tolerate a lot of things from her, but that was a hard no on my part.

"Don't be a dick. I wasn't just 'doing porn.' I was running a fucking business, and it took me a lot of hard work to build my name up in the industry, but now it's trash. I'm a thief. Nobody trusts me. I need to clear my name. The only way I can do that is if I go to the police, explain what happened, and even if I have to do jail time, at the very least everybody will know it was a big mistake on my part."

"No," I said. I didn't even know how to process what she was saying, just that it was a bunch of nonsense. Her heart was in the right place, but she didn't even know what kind of can of worms she was opening. "Just no. To all of that."

She raised her eyebrow and pursed her lips. "You know 'no' doesn't work on me, right? First of all, I don't want to be in porn anymore, so don't be so fucking insecure. There's a million things I can do with my contacts that don't involve showing my tits on the internet. Second of all, you went to jail. You survived…"

"I'm gonna stop you right there," I said. "I went to kid jail. And I'm a man. You're not turning yourself in."

"Do you want me to stay or not? I'm doing this for you, Judas. For our future. I don't want to spend my life looking over my shoulder. I don't want you to have to worry every fucking day that some random guy I owe money to is going to show up and blow your head off. I'm protecting the club as much as I'm protecting myself."

"We've been getting on just fine without your protection," I said. She didn't have the first clue about what she was talking about.

"Why don't you understand? I'm trying to make things right." She stood up from the bed and started tossing her stuff into her backpack, storming through my room like a tornado.

"Where are you going to go?" I asked.

"To Tressica's. She works for a law firm. Maybe her lawyers can help me with my case."

I grabbed her backpack and threw it over my shoulder.

## Judas

I wrapped my arms around her waist and stared down at that beautiful face, stared into those defiant eyes that made me hard and angry at the same time. "Let me take care of it," I said. "It's not you against the world anymore. When you're with me, I promise, I'll give you the life you want." I pressed my lips to her forehead.

"I want more than these four walls, Judas. I want more than a life of waiting around for a phone call from the coroner. I don't want to end up like my mama."

"I'm gonna give you everything, babe. Everything you want. More." I kissed her soft lips, trying to resist my urge to just rip her clothes off. "You gotta trust me."

"The last time a man said that to me I ended up in Vegas selling my ass for money."

"Well, your ass is no longer for sale," I said. "Nobody can own you, Athena. You're bigger than that. And you're totally right, I'd never expect you to just be my old lady."

"Honey, any woman should be honored 'just' to be your old lady. I feel like such a bitch. It's just... it's in my blood. I don't want a man to provide me things that I can provide myself. I want you. I want the man who can give me all the things I never knew I needed." She batted her long eyelashes at me. It was the Athena I fell in love with all those years ago summed up in a single glance. Wild and free. Independent. True outlaw to the point of not being able to even fit in with a biker gang.

"You know what I think we both need right now?" I asked. "We need to go for a ride. When's the last time you been on a bike?"

"Shit, Jude, not since I left home," she said with a shrug. "I didn't just swear off *you* bikers, I swore off all bikers." I don't know why, but it made me feel better. Made me feel like in some twisted way, I still got a part of her that nobody had had. None of those men or women who'd used her body in Vegas. They never got the chance to feel her pressed up against them on the back of a bike, not like I had. Not like I was going to. "Can we go to Parker Dam?"

"Definitely." Parker Dam was the perfect spot for an official first date. Sure, I'd been out there with her a million times before. In the summer, her, Colt, and I used to wander the trails, smoking joints and swimming in the lake. I hadn't been there since my dog Jonny died. I used to take him swimming every chance I got.

"I don't have a bathing suit," she said, raising her eyebrows.

"Neither do I," I teased, swatting her round ass.

The purpose of this trip was twofold. Obviously I wanted to spend the day with her. Any man would be crazy not to. I also needed to get on my bike and clear my mind, try and figure out how I was going to keep my promise to her. I needed to figure out how I was going to keep her safe and get her out of the mess she was in without her ending up dead or in jail. We could only pretend like there wasn't an axe hanging over our heads for so long, and it was only a matter of time before somebody leaked her whereabouts or her affiliation with the club.

I could promise her the world, but if I couldn't deliver, I'd definitely lose her. I knew the clock was ticking. Today we could just live in ignorance, though. Today I was taking my woman to Parker Dam.

## 24

## Athena

I forgot how good it felt to be flying down the winding country roads with the wind on my face and the sun on my back. Never once when I rode with Judas did I ever feel frightened, even though he was kind of a daredevil. He didn't ride the way he did to show off or try and impress me, he did it because he knew that machine inside and out. I wouldn't be surprised if he was doing complicated equations in his brain, calculating the curves of the road and the viscosity of the air. It almost hurt my heart that his brilliance was wasted on the club.

Almost.

Except he was happy. He was content with this life. He had a family. Even though the good lord granted him brains and a body, he had to create that for himself. I couldn't picture him as a lawyer or a doctor. Right now, my arms wrapped firm around his waist, my face pressed into the leather of his cut, I couldn't picture him as anything but this. Couldn't picture myself anywhere else. It was crazy how powerful these machines were.

He parked his bike near the trailhead to the

Quehanna. Camping season was in full swing, and everywhere we walked, people were sitting outside of their RVs and tents, drinking beer out of plastic cups and grilling over little fires. I wondered what they thought as we walked past, him in his boots and leather, me and my porn star aesthetic, hand in hand with shit eating grins across our faces.

Probably that we were the luckiest people to ever exist.

At least, I felt that way.

So many memories of my childhood came rushing back. Nothing smelled like the Pennsylvania Wilds. I had tried to describe it to people in Vegas a million times before, but there weren't really any words for it. We didn't even really have grass there, though. Being out amongst the trees and mountain laurel, the flowing water of a million underground springs, it made you feel so blessed. Like something bigger put all this stuff here just for you. Bigger than the people who put up the casinos and high rise apartments. Bigger than the guy who dug a hole in our yard and plopped in an apple tree because I wanted one. It never really did thrive out there, but that's what happens when you try and use your money to play God.

We walked up to the trailhead, the familiar path of stones that went uphill for about a half mile, crossing streams and twisting through fields of grass that came up to my ass. My flip flops were definitely not made for this, and after a little while, I took them off and shoved them in my pockets, letting my feet feel the earth below me.

He grinned at me like I'd lost my mind. Maybe I had. This was a different kind of intoxication than the one I'd find in a bottle or a pill. The combination of the perfect weather and the man by my side, my heart felt so full, I thought it was going to explode.

"Holy shit," I blurted as we came up on the random

mailbox sticking out of the ground. These 'trail registers' held notebooks of people who had traveled through in the past. Hikers were encouraged to fill out their name, the date they hiked through, and any notes about their hike. I was sure the old register, the one we had filled out a long time ago had since been replaced with a new one, but I couldn't help but open it up and check it out.

There was a plastic bag filled with notebooks, some of them yellowed with age.

Judas sat down on a big boulder, and I sat on his lap, pulling out book after book, thumbing through, reading about all the people who had passed through these very woods. When I got to the book that was dated 2008, my heart skipped a beat. It was silly, but there was something magical about going back in time.

I flipped through it furiously, thinking maybe I'd find a little piece of my past there. A nice memory of Judas and Colt and I. Instead, in big bright red handwriting that could only be my brother's were the words "Athena Jones sucks dick for money."

"It's like he was a fortune teller or something," I blurted out, laughing so hard I couldn't breathe. I could tell Judas was trying to hold in his laughter too. It was cute how he was trying to be respectful, even though I knew we couldn't skirt the topic much longer.

"I'm surprised he spelled all that right," Judas said. I pressed my lips to his. He took the book from my hand and closed it, sliding it back into the bag.

"You know, I really thought maybe there'd be something else in there. These days out here in the woods with you were some of my favorite memories. I guess I never knew as it was happening that that was going to be the case. If I would've known that, I would've definitely written it down."

He turned me around in his lap so I was facing him, straddling him. "For so long, that's all I thought you were ever going to be to me, Athena. A memory. No matter how good it was in the past, it was painful thinking about you. I tortured myself every week watching your show, hoping that it'd make me hate you. Knowing all the people you'd been with, all the shit you'd done when you could've just stayed here with me, it made me feel like shit for never trying to make you stay, but it never made me care about you any less."

He brushed my hair out of my face. He'd seen what I'd done. He'd known me inside and out, and he still didn't think any less of me. The fact that he'd tortured himself for me for years made me feel even worse.

"I don't deserve you," I said. "How'd you turn out so good?"

His laugh was sad, but he took my head in his hands and kissed me passionately. I felt his cock stiffen beneath my leg. "Why would you let a bitch like me ruin you, Judas?"

If I was good at anything in this world, it was ruining a moment.

"Don't say that shit," he said. "You never did anything wrong to me. If anything, I failed you. That day at the club, right before you ran off, right before your old man was killed, I knew you were fixing to leave. He told me you were struggling. I shoulda been better. I shoulda been there. I was too busy worrying about what was going to happen to the MC. I let you slip through the cracks. We all did."

"Ya'll were just kids too. Why do you think Reena and I don't get along. She was supposed to be the adult. She was supposed to make everything okay."

## Judas

"Don't pin that shit on your mama," he said. "She loves you. She loves all of us."

I wasn't going to fight with him about this. He'd lost his parents so long ago, basically raised himself, he didn't understand how hard it was to grow up with two live parents who didn't give a shit about you. All they cared about was the club.

I stood up and dusted off my hands on my shorts. It was getting late and I didn't want to be stuck out here in the dark with no shoes without a flashlight.

"Where ya going?" he asked as I started back towards the trailhead. "Don't you wanna go swimming?"

"The lake is that way."

"We're not going to the lake," he said. "Those tourists were already eyeballing us like we were out here stealing babies and slinging meth. You take off your clothes to go swimming and we're definitely gonna attract some attention. You're supposed to be laying low, anyway."

"Why are you always right?" I whined.

He crouched down in front of me. "Hop on," he said. I looked at him like he was crazy. "I know a place, but I don't think your pedicured toenails are gonna like it too much." I got on his back, and he stepped off the trail to a smaller clearing, mindfully stepping on stones so as to not upset the ferns and wildflowers growing on the forest floor. How could anyone be so thoughtful and still be affiliated with our crew? He never ceased to amaze me. I liked the feeling of being this close to him.

I gasped as we reached a small pond surrounded by giant boulders. It was beautiful. The water was so clear, I could see the minnows swimming around in it.

"I used to bring Jonny out here all the time," he said. "This was his favorite spot."

"Who's Jonny?" I asked. "And did you carry him on your back, too?" He set me down on a rock and began to strip down. I'd never get tired of looking at those abs. Something about his body made me both warm and cold at the same time. I was shivering, but I felt like I was burning up.

"He was a dog I found at one of our demo sites. I think somebody was trying to throw him away, too. He was ugly as hell, had three legs and one good eyeball, but damn I loved that mutt." He grabbed a giant stick and started swirling the water, stepping from stone to stone fully naked, and I tried not to laugh. "Gotta check for rattlesnakes. I never seen any here before, but you gotta be careful this time of year."

"I think somebody is pulling your leg there, Judas," I said. I slid out of my shorts while he continued to stir the pond. He was still working on his project by the time I was stripped down and in the water. It only came up to my knees, and I whooped at the freezing cold temperature. "Snakes don't like being cold."

My eyes grew wide as he fished out a giant black milk snake, setting it down on a rock. It slithered off, and my skin crawled. I forgot what being out in the wild was like. Even though they aren't poisonous, I still didn't want to step on that sucker.

"What happened to Jonny?" I asked, stepping further out into the pond, mindful of what was under my feet.

"He just didn't wake up one day. Vet said there was nothing wrong with him. Just went to sleep one night, and that was it."

"That's sad," I said.

"Maybe," he said, sliding in the water next to me, grunting a little at the cold. "I like to think he just did everything he had to do in this life, and it was his time to go. Lord knows I spoiled the shit out of him."

# Judas

"I bet you did," I said, squeezing his hand. This man would be an amazing dog father. Hell, he'd be an amazing father in general. Call me crazy, but my ovaries twitched at the thought. I wondered if that was something he ever thought about.

"I'd do it again in a heartbeat," he said. "Never really went out of my way to find another one, though. Betty Sue kinda started chewing up all my time."

"Not all stray dogs are good like Jonny," I teased. "Some of them are just bitches. I wish I could've known him."

He stepped a little further into the center of the pond, holding my hand the whole time. The bottom dropped off rather quickly, and soon, I had to hold on to his shoulders to keep my head above the water. The solid flesh of his muscles felt so good pressed against my naked body. It was almost magical being here with him, in a place that nobody knew existed, like he was showing me a special part of his soul. A sacred spot where just him and I could exist. No outsiders, no interruptions, just the two of us at our most vulnerable.

We could make this work. As long as this place existed, this feeling existed, it didn't matter what was going on outside. This was who and what we were meant to be.

We floated around the pond together, swimming, splashing, laughing about old times, not a care in the world. I climbed up on a rock to let what was left of the sun dry my skin, and he parted my thighs, his talented tongue taking me to heights of orgasm that I'd never felt before, my screams ripping through the forest, wild and primal, as I let him explore my most intimate places up close and personal.

He looked over my naked body like he'd just accomplished something monumental as I laid there out of breath and writhing.

"What are you smiling about?" I asked, as I took his hard cock in my my fist, stroking it slowly, watching the precum bead from the tip as he grew more aroused.

"Nothin'," he said with a mischievous chuckle. He laid on top of my body, his face just inches from mine, and slid into my anxious pussy in one hard thrust. My toes curled.

"Fuck, Judas," I moaned. "You feel so good."

"So do you, princess," he said. He started to laugh again as he thrusted in and out slowly, sawing up against my g-spot every time he reentered. I felt that familiar ripple through my walls, and I let go again. He held his dick deep inside of me as my core throbbed around him.

"What is so damn funny?" I cried out through my moans. He slammed his dick in and out of me, and my tender clit could barely take any more. When he reached down and circled it with his fingers, I nearly levitated off the rock. I'd never came so many times in my life before. My brain felt like it was leaking out of my ear. He'd fucked me stupid, and he was laughing the entire time.

I felt his thighs stiffen under my hands, his muscles rippling, and he pulled his dick out and coated my stomach with his hot jizz, nodding in admiration at his accomplishment. He kissed my lips and took me in his arms, dunking me in the cool water and rinsing me off.

"You're a fucking tank, Judas," I sighed, my body feeling like I'd just ran a marathon. He'd taken it all out of me. I needed a nap, a snack, and probably a motor scooter to get around for the next week or two. I rested my head on his chest as we laid on a rock, the air growing colder by the minute.

"You're not so bad yourself," he said. His abs began to ripple underneath my body, and I knew he was cracking up again. "Especially when you're not faking it." He ran his fingertips up and down the soft flesh of my stomach and hugged me tight.

"Is that what's so funny to you?" I said, rolling over to straddle him. His grin was so cocky, so sexy, and he shot me a wink.

"Girl, I've seen you cum at least a thousand times before. Not like this, though."

"Well, duh," I said, pecking his lips. "It's called acting." I let out my loudest porn star moan, my high pitched signature squeal, and collapsed on top of him in a fit of laughter. "Real isn't as pretty."

"I like real," he said, running his fingers through my hair. "Real is more than pretty. Real is perfect."

"Well, I think what we have here is about is real as it gets, Judas. And you earned the right to wear that cocky ass grin you're rocking right now."

He licked his lips and smiled. "Not gonna lie, you stroke my ego just about as good as you stroke my dick." We laid there together until the mosquitos started biting and the sun began to set. The last ten minutes of our hike was in damn near total darkness, and as we fumbled around, gripping on to each other, we laughed like teenagers, wild and free without a single fuck to give even at the campers who suddenly grew very quiet as they saw us walking by.

"You up for dinner?" he asked as he pulled a sweatshirt out of the side bag on his bike and handed it to me. My stomach was growling. I nodded enthusiastically as I pulled the sweatshirt on over my sunburnt and bug bitten body, damn near swimming in it. I didn't care. It smelled like him, like the ultimate comfort surrounding my body, even though he was right here with me. I didn't need to say it.

He didn't need to say it. Thing were good. We were good. This was going to be the new normal.

He straddled his bike, and I followed suit, leaning into him, right where I belonged. Life suddenly got really real for once. If I could trust this man with my body, my mind, my soul, surely I could trust him to make things right. Surely he could keep me safe from the dangers looming over me, right? Certainly this was real enough that we could exist in this world together, no matter what life was going to throw our way.

## 25

## Isaac

"What are you doing out of your room?" I shouted as I caught Betty Sue out of the corner of my eye. "You want me to tie you up again?"

She nearly fucked me over big time last night when she broke out of the closet and called Judas from a burner phone I'd left laying on the coffee table. It took everything in me not to just shut her up for good when I got back to the apartment, but she's worth much more alive than she is dead. Besides, all it took to motivate this broad was a baggie of brown stuff, and she was right back on the same page as I needed her to be.

"I'm hungry," she said. "I smelled food." She cowered in the doorway, and I looked over her skeletal body in admiration at what I'd done. Sure, the track marks on her arms were ugly, but the fingerprints on her neck made my dick twitch in my jeans. I had complete control over this bitch, something my brother never had. He was too busy being a nice guy to break her in good.

I motioned for her to join me on the couch and slid the

plate of what was left of my dinner in front of her, a few scraps of gristle from my steak and the skin of a baked potato. She didn't even bother with silverware, just shoved it in her mouth. I don't even think the bitch bothered to chew. She was officially my pet. Nothing more than a dog. She held her stomach and groaned until she started to dry heave.

"Shouldn't have ate so fast, you idiot," I said with a laugh. She didn't even bother with a comeback, just blinked her dark eyes at me like she knew I was right. Of course I was. I was her keeper.

"Can I please have some water?" she asked. God, she sounded so pathetic. It took everything in me not to bend her over the couch and fuck her raw. I had work to do, though. I handed her a bottle of water, and pulled the baggie out from my pocket. She immediately perked up, nearly salivating at the sight of her beloved heroin.

This would be so much more fun if I could keep her sober, but I didn't feel like messing with the detox part of things. I was going to get to have my fun soon, anyway. Soon as I got these fuckers to start taking me seriously.

Either the men who were on the hunt for Athena, or my brother. Didn't really matter which one at this point, either way I'd finally get what I've been craving all these years. I'd finally break him, too, just like I'd broken his whore.

I leapt from the couch when my phone rang, vibrating across the coffee table. I'd been waiting for this call all day.

"Is that them?" she asked, her voice soft and meek. I stroked the side of her face. She knew all about my plan to hand Athena over. She had no idea she was part of the plan, too. Stupid, stupid, bitch.

I gulped and took a deep breath. I needed to sound as tough as possible. I needed to be in control.

"You got her?" the computer like voice on the other line asked.

"Soon," I said.

## 26

## Judas

"Looks good so far," I said to Colt. He was giving me the grand tour of the Anderson warehouse, and already it was looking a lot better than the feral cat infested squatter house it had been when we bought it. The parking lot was lined with overflowing dumpsters and piles of scrap metal. It was basically only wall to wall concrete inside now. Part of me felt a little guilty for not being around to lend a hand today, especially as Vice President.

Part of me didn't give a single fuck, because this day with Athena was one of the best days of my life in a long time. Maybe ever. The only thing I wanted now was more of those days. The only thing I needed now was a way to make sure we could stay this way forever without having to worry about her turning herself in or getting capped by some assholes she owed money to.

If I couldn't uphold my end of the deal, take care of this problem, make it go away, I knew I was gonna lose her.

"Check this out, bro," Colt said, leading me to furthest back corner of the building. He swung open a heavy steel door, and I patted him on the back, admiring the handiwork of my brothers.

"That's real nice," I said. The floor was concrete, a drain running down the middle. The walls were tile. There was a huge steel basin sink in the corner and a hose hung from the ceiling. "We can have some serious fun in this room. No more of this peasant shit having to lug around clean up kits everywhere we go." Yeah, it was a torture room. A murder room. A room nobody would ever want to find themselves in.

He swung open the emergency exit door and motioned for me. "Yeah, but look at this shit." Rosey was taking a backhoe to the dirt out back. Breaker and Miles were pounding posts into the ground. "Moses is getting a new home," he said. "Gonna put a retractable roof on this sucker, upgrade his baby pool into a pond, maybe get him a girlfriend."

"I like that," I said. The club knew how I felt about keeping a fucking alligator in the house. It wasn't fair to him. Besides, our stupid drunk asses didn't need the temptation. I don't know how many times somebody wanted to take him out and play with him or show him off to some bitch to try and impress her. This warehouse was strictly work, and Moses would definitely be an asset, especially when some dumb fool tried to get out via the emergency exit. Colt was kind of a sick fucker, but I liked his style.

"How'd you shake the skank?" he asked, lighting up a cigarette. "After the way she was acting last night I figured she'd be wedged so far up your asshole you'd never even get to take a shit in private again."

"She got a sunburn," I said. Tressica was at the house when we got back, and they wanted to catch up. Didn't realize that entailed eating ice cream in my bed and watching some shitty show about teenage moms, but seeing her happy was worth it.

"I didn't know plastic burnt," he said. "Figured it just melted."

"You can be a dick to her face. I know that's your weird sibling bonding shit, but I don't want to hear it anymore. I don't ride your sack about your fucking situation." He nodded at me and put his hands up in the air. "We need to talk about how we're going to handle this by the way. Is everybody here?"

"None of ya'll need to handle it," he said. "I'm just gonna wait for shit to blow up in my face."

"Not your situation," I said. Nobody wanted to touch his situation with a ten foot pole. "I mean Athena. We need to handle it. We need to make it go away."

"I told you my solution," he said with a shrug. "Hand the bitch over." I knew he was just kidding but I was getting sick of it. This wasn't a joke. This was her life. Mine and her life. The club was in danger, too, once word got out that she was hanging around here. "I thought she was just gonna run off to Montana anyway. What, you got that magic dick or something?" He tapped me in the cock and I clenched my fist.

"Knock it off, asshole," I said. "These men could be closing in on us at any time. I don't want to lose a brother because we didn't handle our shit. It's what we do. I don't want us to have to live in constant fear. I don't want us to let our guard down one day and get fucking mauled like your old man and the rest of the crew. This needs to end. Tomorrow."

"Relax," Colt said. "While you guys were out screwing around all day, Law and Sharky were taking care of business." We walked into the office, and I was amazed at the set up. There were computer monitors everywhere, camera surveillance on every inch of the building inside and out. Sharky was tapping away at the keyboard and on screen was a bunch of random code that looked like gibberish to me. The air was thick with pot smoke, and I felt like I was being fishbowled in. He was a strange prospect, skinny little nerdy dude who lived in his momma's basement, but he knew more about computers than all of us put together. Plus, the young buck could tear down an engine and put it back together in record speed.

"How's it coming along?" Colt asked.

"I need her original computer," he said, dropping his head to the keyboard. "I'm fucking failing here."

Law was watching over his shoulder, squinting his eyes, trying to make sense of the code. "Yeah, none of this is anything I can feed into my databases. I already hit up all my sources. These people are operating on anonymous servers all over the world. I need names. Even aliases." We never specifically asked Law what organization he worked for when he patched in, all we knew was that he had some major connections. It was a secret we were willing to let him keep in exchange for the access he had. At this point we had enough collateral on him to fuck up anything he had going on if in fact he was undercover, but none of us ever doubted his loyalty for a minute.

"You get her original computer and we can get this shit figured out?" I asked. "Easy as that?"

"Dude, you know it's never easy as that," Law said. "But it'd make things a lot easier."

"So, we're going to Vegas?" I asked.

Law groaned. "You people know I fucking hate Vegas. But yeah, let's do it. We can fly out in the morning, be back by Friday. I'll make some calls and get us set up just in case we need back up. I think you and I can handle it."

We gathered the rest of the brothers and went over the

plan. Law and I were going to go get the computer. Everyone else was on Athena watch. I'd already taken enough risks getting her out of the house today. It wasn't like she blended in with a crowd. If everything went as planned, by the end of the weekend she could do whatever she pleased wherever she pleased.

"You're not gonna tell her, are ya?" Colt asked.

I shrugged and stared at my boots. I probably shouldn't. I knew she wasn't going to be thrilled at the idea of me going back to her old stomping grounds and busting heads. Most guys didn't keep their old ladies in the loop when it came to club business. It was easier that way. I wasn't most guys.

And Athena wasn't the average old lady. She made that very clear. If I couldn't be honest with the woman I loved, we'd never be able to make it. Once you started sneaking around about one thing, shit always started to unravel.

"I'm gonna go pack," I said. "See ya'll in the morning?" If I was going to be on the road for the rest of the week, I wanted her to myself for the rest of the night.

"I'll pick you up at eight," Law said. I loved these guys more than I had words for, more than family. Sure, we were doing this for Athena, we all had a thing for damaged damsels in distress, but I knew they were doing this as much for me. Just as I would do for them. Our brotherhood was more than just some letters on a vest and fast and loud bikes.

"You heard from Isaac today?" Colt asked as he walked me out to the parking lot.

"Nah." He and I didn't talk every day unless it was club related. After that weird Betty Sue call last night, I'm sure he was just hiding at home licking his wounds.

"Me neither. He was supposed to do the dumpsters today. Fucker ain't answering his phone."

"Boot him out," I said. "I'm not playing his games anymore. I don't care if he has a bone to pick with me, if he can't do the shit he needs to do for the club, he doesn't have a place here." Maybe it was a pussy move on my part, giving him the okay while I was going to be out of town, but I didn't need him meddling in my shit, trying to get under my skin. Him and Betty Sue could fuck right off.

"Fair enough," Colt said. "I'll see ya in the morning. Drive safe, brother."

He patted me on the back. "You want me to give your sister a kiss for you?"

"Fuck you," he said, shaking his head. "How long you been saving that one for?"

He knew as much as I did. I'd been saving that line my whole life, and now I was finally getting the chance to live out that dream. I hopped on my bike and made my way back to the clubhouse.

## 27

## Judas

"You smell guilty," she said to me as I slid under the covers next to her. I wasn't trying to wake her, but her naked flesh was too much for me to handle, and she snapped awake the second I spooned up right next to her.

"Only person who touched my dick was Colt, I swear," I said with a laugh. "And it wasn't in a sexy way, obviously."

She rolled over to face me. "That's why you smell guilty. What are you scheming?"

"We're not scheming shit. We're gonna go take care of your situation. Sharky and Law need your computer and we're gonna go get it." She sat bolt upright, flicking on the lamp on the nightstand. Even with squinted sleepy eyes and no make up, she was the most beautiful sight I could've possibly imagined. Even with a scowl on her face and rage in her eyes.

"I'll do it," she said. "You guys don't know what you're getting into. I know how to handle Harold better than ya'll do. I can charm whatever I want out of that man."

I never wanted to think about her doing anything with

that man ever again. Half the reason why I wanted to go was so that I could let him know exactly how I felt about him.

"You miss him or something?" I asked, anger stirring in my stomach.

"Judas, you gotta quit with this insecurity shit," she said. "I don't give a fuck about him. I just don't want you guys going in there making a scene and ruining my reputation."

"Your reputation?" I snapped. "Right now you don't have a reputation to defend. You have a fucking target on your back. There is literally a bounty on your head. You did this, Athena. Now let me do what I do."

She put her head in her hands and began to sob. My heart hurt. I went too far. I never wanted to make this woman cry. I wanted to help her. All I was doing was making things worse. I wrapped my arm around her shoulder and she leaned into my body and wailed.

"I know I did this," she said. "I didn't think it would end up like this, though. I just wanted better for my life. I just wanted something for me. I was being so selfish. I don't want anybody to get hurt because of my stupid actions."

I felt her words. I felt her circumstance. I knew she never meant any harm to anybody. She was desperate. Things got out of hand. I knew I didn't have the right thing to say, so I just let her cry it out in my arms.

"Nobody's gonna get hurt," I finally said as she started to settle down. "I'm sure we can work something out. These guys are all big and bad behind their keyboards, but I'm sure as soon as we find out who they are, we can come up with a deal." I knew I promised myself I wasn't going to lie to her. I knew people *were* probably going to get hurt. I knew I was heading down a slippery slope, a line I never wanted to even toe.

"Sounds nice, Judas, but I know you're full of shit."

She sunk her head back in the pillow and groaned. "Can I please just go to jail?"

"Listen, babe," I said. "I know what you grew up with. I know how your old man operated. Things are different. Nobody gets hurt unless they have to get hurt. I promise I will do whatever I can to reason, beg, borrow, barter, whatever. Hurting anybody is worse case scenario."

"I don't want *you* to get hurt," she said, reaching for my hand. "I don't care what happens to anybody else."

"What about your reputation?" I asked, tracing my hand up her thigh. I watched her shiver under my touch.

Her lips puckered into a sly smile. "When have you ever known me to care about my reputation?"

"So you're full of shit, too," I said, tracing my fingers further and further up her flesh as she squirmed.

"That's how you know you met your match," she giggled. "When you find somebody willing to call you on your shit."

"Get over here," I said, pulling her on to my lap. It didn't take much for her to make me rock hard, hell, the smell of her hair alone was enough to make me cum in my jeans in public. Her pussy wrapped around my cock like a glove, wet and ready for me, the thought of her laying here naked under the covers waiting for me while I was gone damn near making me lose my load the very second. She was so perfect. So mine. I thrust my hips to the rhythm of her rocking, pulling her down on me harder and harder while her moans filled the room.

"You know the only thing that could hurt me would be losing you," I said, digging my fingers into the flesh of her hips, holding her on my cock as she writhed and arched her back. Her walls throbbed around me, the warm familiar gush of her cumming on top of me only making me want to fuck her harder.

"You'll always have me," she moaned, her hungry lips reaching for mine. I drove my tongue into her mouth as I exploded inside of her, filling her with my seed. She purred as I wrapped my arms around her, my hands running over the perfect flesh of her ass.

"Then you let me do what I need to do," I said. As much as it pained me to leave her. As much as I wanted to just blink and all our problems would be solved. As much as I hated knowing what the next few days could bring for me, my club, for her. "You let me do what I need to do, and you don't leave the walls of this clubhouse til I get back."

"What, are you grounding me?" she asked, raising her eyebrows in defiance.

"Do I need to tie you up and spank you?"

"I mean, you can," she said with a wink. "When you get back from Vegas."

I breathed a sigh of relief as I softened inside of her. I kissed her forehead, running my fingers through that perfect mess of blonde hair. We were on the same page. Same wavelength.

"You know I'm only doing this cuz I love you," I said, biting my lip.

"You know I'm only letting you do this because I love you more," she sighed. "I swore I'd never come back to this place, let alone be somebody's old lady, but in my heart, I knew if it was ever going to happen, it was gonna be all your fault."

"Yeah, well, once we get this shit straightened out, we won't be staying here at the clubhouse anymore. I'm not gonna let you go to Montana, but I got my eye on a farmhouse about ten miles up the road you might like." She smiled at me, her eyes glowing. "I'm not much of a cowboy, but I can try."

"How'd you know about my cowboy thing?"

"Your momma talks about you a lot more than you'd believe."

She rolled over on the bed and let out a loud laugh. "Can you promise me you'll never say anything about my mom again while your dick is inside me?"

"Fair enough," I laughed. I reached for the lamp, and held her in my arms until we both passed out. This was by far the best day of my life. I could only hope that the next few would ensure this was how I was going to live the rest of the days of my life.

## 28

## Athena

I'd been on lockdown before. As a kid, it was always kind of exciting. Momma and the other old ladies would spend all day in the kitchen baking and cooking like they were getting ready for Christmas dinner, and us kids would hang out in a spare bedroom eating snacks, watching movies, and building pillow forts. It's sad that some of the best memories of my early life were of times when all the adults around me were fearing for theirs. They never let on like that was the case. The mood was always light for the most part. After a few days, the men would start getting sick of each other, and fights would break out, but it never bothered me. I got to skip school and be around my friends and family. It was an ideal situation for a child.

As an adult, it was definitely not nearly as fun. Especially because I was the reason we were on lock down. Especially because the only people locked down were myself and my mother, and the revolving door of Indignants who were tasked with making sure I didn't make a break for it.

I was going mildly insane, wondering what the hell was

taking Judas so long to reply to my texts. I knew they had touched down in Vegas. I knew they had checked into the hotel. Other than that, I was completely in the dark. I decided to take it out on the filthy pig sty the clubhouse had turned into.

"Can you stop for like five fucking minutes?" my mother asked, hovering over me as I scrubbed the baseboards of the bar room on my hands and knees.

"This place is disgusting," I said. "Just cuz ya'll are a bunch of garbage men doesn't mean you have to live in filth. Why the hell do you even have prospects if they're not keeping up with the chores?"

I shot Isaac a look of death, but he just smiled at me and went back to playing on his phone. I had half a mind to smack that smug smile off his face. I could let it slide that Judas tolerated his shit, he's a better person than I am, but my brother must've been getting soft in his old age. Soft, or way too busy juggling bitches.

"Athena Jones," my mother scolded, "I know you think you're better than all of us, but you need to check your attitude. So sorry this place isn't up to your standards. Would you be more comfortable if we laid down a tarp covered in lube and brought in a camera crew?"

I spat on the floor and got up from my hands and knees, throwing my rag blackened with dirt in her face.

"Baby, stop," she said, chasing after me as I headed for the door. "I'm sorry. I'm just stressed. My back's been killing me lately, and the doctor won't give me any more of them good pills til I go to physical therapy. Shit's just been slipping." She looked so guilty, like I'd just jammed a sword through her pride. I'd never seen my mother this close to tears in my whole life.

"Mama what?" I asked softly. I reached for her hand.

# Judas

Everyone in the room was staring at us. She burst into tears and took off for the kitchen.

"Real nice, Athena," Elaine said, rolling her eyes at me. She immediately went back to filing her nails and watching whatever trash talk show was on the TV above the bar.

"Ya'll should be ashamed of yourselves!" I shouted. "That's a broken woman, and you all are too fucking thick to know any better. When's the last time any of you even thanked her for picking up after your asses or feeding you?"

"Oh, get off your high horse, hon," Elaine said. "Not like you been here to pitch in. You just roll in whenever you feel like it and everybody's supposed to bow down to your whims. No wonder nobody cared when you left." This bitch, I knew she was speaking the mind of all the sluts hanging around the MC. I almost couldn't be mad about it because she was just doing what club sluts do. I couldn't let it slide though.

Between worrying about Judas and now my mother, too, my nerves were fried as fuck. Nothing a good old fashioned beat down couldn't fix. I started to take out my earrings as I stared into her eyes. She didn't even show a hint of fear, just sat there on the couch, casually filing away at her nails.

She held up her middle finger and began to sharpen it into a pencil sharp point.

The front door swung open, and everyone immediately either dropped to the floor or reached for their pistols.

"Nice, nice," Colt said, putting his hands in the air and laughing. "You guys got them cat like reflexes."

"Dammit, Colt," Delaney growled. "Your timing is shit. Your sister and Elaine were about to slap the shit out of each other."

"Don't let me stop ya," Colt said. "You want this?" He

reached in his holster and offered Elaine his pistol. I punched him in the stomach on my way to the kitchen.

Mama was sitting on the floor, her back up against the dishwasher. She looked up at me with mascara running down her face, and quickly began to wipe her eyes. As she tried to push herself off the linoleum, she groaned in pain. She looked so pathetic sitting there. So tiny and fragile. It made me sick to my stomach.

"You need to tell me what's going on," I said, sitting down next to her, taking her hand in mine.

"You wouldn't understand," she said. "I raised you better than to understand."

"What's wrong with your back?" I asked. I knew whatever the issue was was much deeper than a back ache, but I figured I'd start with the tip of the iceberg.

"I don't know, Athena," she said. "I think I pulled a muscle. I just figured it'd heal on its own. I don't have time to do all that doctor shit."

"You got all the time in the world, mom. You got all the money in the world. You got people around you who care about you and will take your anywhere you need to go. That's a terrible excuse."

"I just can't, Athena. You wouldn't get it. Ever since your daddy died, I been lost. This place isn't the place I came up in. There's no room for me here. The only role I have is mom. If I can't look after these boys and clean up after them, they got no use for me. This is the only life I know. I start being a nuisance and I'm out on the street. I have nothing."

She began to sob, and for the first time in my life, I was ready to admit how badly I felt for her. I had a hard time understanding her parenting style. I spent many long nights wondering why we never had a relationship like most mothers and daughters. I thought she was so weak for

# Judas

letting men walk all over her her entire life. She wasn't weak. She just didn't know any better, and now, she was killing herself for everybody else's benefit.

"You kids hate me, but you don't understand, I raised you the way I did so you wouldn't end up like me. I let you alone so you could learn to be tough. I wanted to push you away. It was better that way."

"I don't hate you," I said, stroking her graying hair. "I never hated you. And you're not everybody's maid. You're royalty, mom. Without you and daddy, this club would've never existed. You should be treated like a queen."

"You're so much like your brother," she said with pained laugh.

I rolled my eyes. "Gross."

"I'm sorry I pushed you away. I'm glad you're back, even if it's under shitty circumstances. Hopefully this will all blow over quick and you can get back to your cowboy chasing."

"I'm not going anywhere, mama," I said. There was no turning back. My five year plan had taken an unexpected plan, and hearing it out loud, off my own lips didn't sound like admitting defeat anymore. It sounded like a sigh of relief. "This is where I want to be."

"He's a good man," she said. "Best man, even. The love he's had for you and your brother ever since we took him in, his loyalty to me and your daddy and this club, the Lord don't make men like that too often."

I knew it. I felt it. I felt it so hard it was almost painful, knowing where he was right now and what he was doing. If I was going to be an old lady, I had a lot to learn from this pro sitting on the floor in front of me.

"How'd you deal with it?" I asked. "Knowing what daddy was up to. How'd you not go crazy worrying sick about him all the time?"

She rested her head on my shoulder. "I guess it was one part trust, one part prayer, and honestly, a whole lot of Jack Daniels. Living in the dark was a lot easier than facing the truth. Little bit of innocence, little bit of ignorance. That's not you, though. This isn't the olden days. You're a lot smarter than I was when I was your age. Not more experienced, though, believe it or not, if ya know what I'm saying," she teased, raising her eyebrows.

"Let's not ever talk about that again, mom. And no more pills for you. Unless the doctor says so. Promise? And you tell these sluts and prospects you're not their maid. Ass, cash, or pick up trash, no free rides here."

"I love you, kid," she said with a laugh. I grabbed her by the hand to help her off the floor, when all of a sudden, a crash came thumping through the wall on the other side of the kitchen. It sounded like liquor bottles from the bar were all falling to the floor, glass shattering everywhere. Muffled shouting came through the wall. I leapt up and ran to the doorway, peeking around the corner.

"What the fuck?" I stammered. Rosey and Miles were holding Isaac on either side of his arms as he tried to run out the doorway. My brother was helping Delaney up off the floor from behind the bar.

"You don't know who you're fucking with!" Isaac was shouting. "You'll see. You'll all see."

He sounded so cheesy and ridiculous, like the kind of villain in an old timey movie who ties girls to the railroad tracks. I didn't know how any of these guys were keeping a straight face. I wasn't sure how he even managed to get Delaney on the floor unless he was completely blindsided.

"It was all Judas," he screamed. "I knew it. Too big of a pussy to tell me himself. You guys had it out for me since day one."

"Judas was the only motherfucker outta all of us who

even wanted you here," Colt said. "He's the only reason why you lasted so long. If it were up to me I'd've never let you anywhere near this club, you piece of shit. After what you did to him? You're a fucking snitch by design."

I hadn't seen my brother this pissed off in a long time, maybe ever. His nostrils flared and he clenched his fists. I wondered what had went down that it was finally time for Isaac to go. It wasn't any of my business. I was just happy it was happening. One less person for Judas to have to keep track of and worry about.

"You just go back to playing house with Betty Sue. I don't wanna see you around here anymore," Colt said. "If you want to discuss this any further, we can take it out back." Colt towered over him and he put his hands in front of his face, cowering in fear. Rosey and Miles walked him out to the parking lot, and Colt paced straight for the bar and grabbed a bottle of beer, chugging it down in one gulp before slamming it on the countertop.

"That went a lot smoother than it normally does?" I said in a soft voice, breaking the silence. I'd only ever known of two prospects who didn't make it through, but they definitely didn't walk out of the building upright.

"Fucking Judas," he said, shaking his head. "If it were up to me, I'd have fed him to Moses just for the fun of it."

"I'm not trying to stick my nose where it don't belong," I said softly, hoping only he could hear me. "But that's a man who likes to run his mouth and has nothing to lose. He's a liability, Colt. What's stopping him from getting in his truck and going straight to the police station?"

"Don't worry yourself," he said. "I got eyes on him til Judas gets back in town."

I just shrugged. I knew it wasn't any of my business, but I had a bad feeling about what had just went down. This day as a whole was overwhelming. At least I knew I was safe in the confines of the clubhouse, and it was going to be nice not having to look at Isaac's ugly face for the duration.

"Did you hear anything from them yet?" I asked. He shook his head.

"Can someone please help me up?" Delaney groaned. He was still laying on the floor in a puddle of liquor and broken glass, and he looked like he was pretty badly cut up.

"Isaac did this to you?" I asked, as Colt and I pulled him up out of the mess and I started to dust him off. "He's like half your size."

"Fucker tripped me," he said, his face turning red with embarrassment.

"You're lucky you didn't fall on your gun and shoot your guts out," Colt said. "That'd be one hell of a glorious mess to clean up."

My mom was standing in the doorway soaking it all in. She had a broom in one hand and a sad smile on her face. I pointed my finger at her and mouthed, "no." She winked at me as she handed the broom to Colt.

"The fuck is this?" he asked.

"I know you've probably never held one before, son, but this is called a broom."

He looked at her with a twisted grin.

"I figure since we're all stuck here today, I can teach you all the wonders of cleaning up after yourselves."

He started cracking up, and everyone followed suit. "Hell yeah," Rosey said, "Mama Reena finally grew a set."

"Oh honey, I've got bigger balls than all ya'll combined. I just don't wanna whip em out and make ya feel inferior." I gagged in my mouth a little bit, as I wrapped my arms around her. "Your maid has officially retired."

Everyone began to clap as she took a bow. I could see

in her eyes how hard this was for her, but she was going to be alright. She'd lived her life for the MC for so long, it was time for her to go do something for herself. "Do you know anything about online dating?" she asked me.

My eyes lit up. That sounded like a perfect way to get my mind off today, playing dress up with my mom, having a photo shoot, and setting up an online dating profile for her. I nodded excitedly, grabbing her by the hand and heading for the hallway.

"You're not going out with any man until I approve of them first," Colt said. "I don't want my new dad to be just any random scumbag."

"Baby, I'm pretty sure I'm done with men. How do you feel about a new mom?"

"I approve!" Rosey shouted. The expression on Colt's face was priceless. Maybe my mom and I didn't have a lot in common, but fucking with him would always be a common bond we shared. Maybe her and I would never have your normal mother daughter bond, but the more time I spent here, the more I realized that normal wasn't what I was built for. No matter how far away I ran from the MC, this was always going to be my final destination.

The cellphone buzzed in my pocket and I groaned, half thrilled to hear from him, half dreading what was about to go down on his end.

*"Going to get it now. Love u."*

I sent him back a kissy face. *"U better come back here in one piece."*

"You alright?" Mom asked as I unlocked the bedroom door.

"Gonna have to be, right? Little bit ignorant, a little bit innocent?"

"How bout that Jack Daniels?" I said with a laugh, heading straight for the cabinet.

## 29

## Isaac

"Wake up!" I shouted to Betty Sue. She was sprawled across my couch, face down in a pillow. She swatted at me and moaned. "Come on, bitch. We gotta go."

This was some fucking bullshit timing. Tonight was the night I was supposed to hand over Athena, and I just got kicked out of the club. Colt used some bullshit bitch ass excuse about me not showing up to work yesterday, but I knew Judas had something to do with it. That pathetic bastard didn't even have the balls to do it himself. He had to have his best friend do it while he was out of town.

I was royally fucked. If I couldn't get Athena out of the clubhouse, I was going to be a dead man. My cellphone kept blowing up, texts from my guy asking for pictures of her. I could only avoid them for so much longer.

"Where we going?" Betty Sue whined. "You're not taking me back to the home are you?"

"No sweetie." I grabbed her by the arm. "It's time." Her eyes lit up from their normal dark and deadened state. This bitch truly was delusional. I felt like a god knowing I made her this way.

## Judas

"We're going to get the money and run away?" I walked her into the bathroom and started the water running on the bathtub. I couldn't sell her in this state. She smelled like stale cigarettes and her hair was coated in grease.

She stripped out of her shorts and tank top. I had to hold in my laughter, knowing that if I punched her in the ribs right now, I could probably shatter all her bones. *Weak, stupid bitch.* I had to control myself. She was much more valuable alive than dead. At this current rate, I'd probably have to use her as a sacrifice anyway to buy myself some more time, to try and figure out how I was going to con Athena into going with me. Maybe I could find a way to drug her. I looked enough like my twin brother, Betty Sue had told me this before. Wouldn't that be something? Slipping in bed with Athena, having my way with that sweet pussy, tricking her before convincing her to go with me. That'd be some epic shit. Then all those assholes would really know who was in charge. Judas'd probably kill himself. My life would be complete.

"Hot," she whined as she dipped her toe in the tub. "Too hot."

"Shut up," I growled. She was fucking up my fantasy with her complaining. I shoved her in the bathtub and she screamed like a drowning cat. Hadn't heard that sound in awhile. It kinda made me halfway hard. My phone rang in my pocket and I tossed her a bar of soap. "Wash your nasty ass. You're making me sick."

I stepped out into the hallway, pacing back and forth, trying to pump myself up so I didn't sound like a little bitch when I answered the call. My heart was pounding. Maybe I wasn't cut out for this after all. It was too late. There was no turning back.

"Where are you?" the chilling voice on the other line asked. "We don't have all day, man."

"I'm working on it," I said. "You're gonna have to give me some time." As soon as I got Betty Sue ready, I'd dump her off as collateral and we could go from there. "Little hitch in the plan, but I got something to hold you over in the meanwhile."

"What the fuck is that supposed to mean?" the man shouted so loud, it damn near blew out my eardrums.

"Yeah, Isaac. What the fuck is that supposed to mean?" Betty Sue stood in front of me, holding my pistol in her quivering hands.

"Jesus Christ, woman, what are you doing?" I stammered. Her eyes were wild, and she pulled the trigger to nothing but a click. I couldn't help but smile at the look of terror on her face.

"You stupid fucking bitch. You think I'd leave a loaded gun laying around your junkie ass?" She took off like a maniac, sprinting for the door, screaming at the top of her lungs the entire time. I chased after her down the hallway of my apartment complex, but stopped in my tracks when I realized we weren't alone.

"Please!" she was screaming. "Help me! Help me!"

Doors were flying open left and right, people gathering outside to see what the commotion was all about.

"She's fucking nuts!" I shouted. "She lost her damn mind. She's high as a kite!"

"He's trying to kidnap me!" she squealed as she sprinted down the steps. "Somebody call the cops!"

*Nobody's gonna take her seriously, dude,* I reminded myself. She was buck ass naked, covered in track marks, and waving a gun around.

"Nothin to see, folks," I said. "Cops are on the way. Go the fuck inside and mind your business." Maybe they weren't, but I'm sure they would be soon. I needed to get the fuck out of here, and fast. I needed to disappear. The police coming after me were the least of my concerns. This little distraction was going to make my ultimate delivery that much harder to pull off.

I walked back into my apartment and started stuffing my things in my backpack. I took one last look over my bedroom, making sure I had all my cash and weapons. I peeked out the window, trying to figure out if it would be better for me to take the fire escape or to just walk out the front door like nothing was going on.

She was getting in a big black truck. I gulped when I recognized the driver and the passenger. Of course those assholes had eyes on me. They knew they couldn't just kick me to the curb and expect me to walk away quietly with my hands between my legs. Kinda gave me a sense of pride for once. My brother and his buddies had to babysit me. I was a dangerous man.

Pride wasn't going to get my out of this building in one piece though. I watched as Breaker got out of the truck. He felt for his waistband and headed for the building. I grabbed my backpack, climbed out the window, and ran down the fire escape. I didn't stop running til my lungs burned and my legs started to cramp. I sat down on a park bench and pulled my hoodie up over my head, trying to catch my breath.

My phone started to ring, and I hit the silence button. I needed a minute to regroup. Maybe my initial plan had been foiled. If I didn't want to end up dead in a ditch somewhere, I needed to figure out a plan, and fast.

## 30

## Judas

Law and I sat in the rental car in front of the ranch style house, looking for signs of movement through the windows. The sun was starting to set over the city, and as the lights began to flicker on in the house where Athena used to live, the shadows of what looked like a man and a woman moved from room to room behind the curtains.

"You gonna be able to be cool in there?" Law asked. I didn't know who he got the guns we were carrying from, just that he was in that shitty apartment complex for a long time and I had to stay in the car. My legs were cramped and my back was sore from traveling all day. We were on a mission. We hadn't even checked into our hotel yet. I wasn't going to be able to chill until I knew we took care of this shit. Law wasn't going to be able to chill even after we did. He wasn't exactly the kind of guy who ever let his guard down. I'm pretty sure the dude slept with one eye open.

"Why would you even ask that?" My voice came out a little weaker than I expected. I was more nervous inside than I'd ever been in my life, and apparently it was showing. This would be the first time I ever met Harold, the man who took my lady away, the man who exploited her when she was too young to know any better. We needed to play nice with him to get what we wanted, but for the first time in a long time, I wasn't sure I had it in me to keep my temper in check and just get the job done.

"You're shakin' like a leaf, dude. Your skin looks gray. You haven't said two words since we touched down. I know you, Judas, and this ain't you. I don't feel good about this if you can't get your shit together." I couldn't stop thinking about Athena and all the shit Harold put her through. One of the earliest episodes of her cam show, where he did a Q&A about 'training' her to be the perfect porn star, the way he talked about her like a piece of meat, laughing and rolling his mustache between his fingers, it still shook me to his day. I wanted to punch him right in the face then. That feeling definitely hadn't left me, even though I knew she was mine now, and I could treat her like the queen was was.

I needed to get my head straight.

I was doing this for her and only her. Doing this so we could have the life we deserved together without ever having to worry about these people again.

"I'm fine," I said. "Just fucking car sick."

He stared right through me with his dark eyes. I knew I couldn't bullshit him.

"This ain't about your feelings, Judas."

"Got it," I said, throwing him a salute, my weak attempt at being convincing as possible.

We got out of the car and crept around the back of the house, crouching down low in the shrubs. I grabbed the handle on the back door, and nodded to Law when I discovered it was unlocked. We walked right into the house, casually and quietly. I was going to keep a look out while Law looked around. He knew the floor plan from the day they busted Athena out.

I stood in the hallway that connected the kitchen and the rest of the rooms. The muffled sound of the television rang from the living room, and I could hear Harold's stupid laugh sporadically. It made my skin crawl.

Against my better judgement, I peeked around the corner. Sprawled out on the couch next to him was a girl who didn't quite look legal. Her hair was bleached blonde and the way her makeup was done instantly reminded me of a young version of Athena. I damn near puked in my mouth.

"I got nothing," Law whispered. "Room's cleaned out."

I pointed to the girl, and he shook his head.

It was time to confront this fucker.

"Put your hands up," I shouted, stepping into the living room, pointing my pistol straight at Harold. The girl began to scream, and like the true pussy he was, he jumped up from the couch and held her in front of him like a shield.

"Oh for fucks' sake. Not you idiots again," he said.

"Oh, I'm not one of the original idiots," I said. I paced closer towards him, my gun trained on his head the entire time. "You don't know me, Harold, but I know you. I know you very well, and I'm the stuff your nightmares are made of." I pushed the barrel of my pistol right into his forehead. "Drop the girl."

The skinny little blonde fell to the ground and began wailing. She crawled across the room in record speed, kneeling at Law's feet. "Please Mister," she pleaded, her French Canadian accent thick. "I won't say anything to anyone. I just wanna go home and see my parents."

"You're fine," he said to her. Two words from his mouth was all it ever took to calm the bitches down. I wished his voice had that effect on me, because my hands were shivering, and it took everything in me not to cap this motherfucker right here.

"Where's Athena's computer?" I asked, poking the gun into his skull just a little bit for emphasis.

"You're kidding, right?" he asked. "Russians came and ripped this place up two days after she left. I gave em everything she left."

I kicked him in the knee. It seemed like a better option than shooting him in the head, even though I desperately wanted to. He fell to the floor, grabbing for his shin. "After everything she'd done for you all those years, that's the kind of loyalty you have? Just hand her over to people who are looking to kill her?"

"Loyalty? Fuck loyalty. She was stealing from me. She was stealing from them. You think you gentlemen are scary, try dealing with a pissed off Russian mafia boss who's son's inheritance got stolen by a porn star. It was self preservation. You'd do the same thing in my shoes. She was gone. I had no other choice." I looked down at him in disgust as he started to cry.

"That's the difference between you and I, Harold. It doesn't matter what Athena does, I'll always love her. I'll always have her back."

"Oh, son," he said shaking his head, "love doesn't even start to factor into the equation. Of course I loved her, I love all my girls, but this is business." He was full blown sobbing by now. I didn't know if he thought he was going to find compassion from me, but the more he ran his mouth, the angrier I got.

"Don't let him fool you," the girl shouted. "he made a deal with the devil. He did this all himself. That's how I ended up here. He sold her out in exchange for me." She was holding on to Law's leg like a fucking spider monkey as she screamed at Harold.

"You lie, bitch," Harold yelled. "I rescued you, and don't you ever forget it."

I locked eyes with Law, and he gave me the nod.

"You're full of shit, Harold," I said, knocking him back down onto the ground. "Now you're gonna pay. You think Athena stole from you? You took things from her that all the cash in the world couldn't buy back. Now this poor fucking girl?" He held his hands up in front of his face, but I brushed them away with my boot, stomping down on his left fingers as I listened to them crunch, like music to my ear. I wanted him to look me in the eyes when I talked to him. He didn't deserve to hide behind his hands, a computer screen, a harem of women who were too young to know any better any longer.

"Ya'll want to give me a minute?" I asked Law.

"Take all the time you need, brother," he said with a wink. He and the girl walked out the back door, and I paused a second, relishing all the things I was going to get to do to this piece of shit.

I knew I promised Athena nobody was going to get hurt.

Sometimes you have to break a couple promises for the greater good.

Besides, I wasn't going to kill him all the way.

I'd let nature decide whether he lives or dies. He thinks the loyalty of my MC is something funny, something cute? If any one of my brothers ever found themselves in his position, one of us would have his back in a heartbeat.

"Where's your mafia buddies now?" I asked, as I pulled a pair of black gloves out of my pocket and slipped them on over my hands. "Where's all your business partners?"

He tried to stand up, but before he could get his balance, I was in the zone, beating him over the head with a table lamp. I flipped couches. I threw tables. I punched holes in the drywall. He thinks the Russians turned the place upside down? I was going to leave his house in complete shambles while he bled out on the white carpet. Years and years of bottled up rage poured through me. Every time my fist made contact with his face or a vase, I felt like I was fucking him as hard as he fucked Athena. I could've gone all day.

Then, my phone rang.

It was her, calling from that random burner. Knowing she was looking for me brought me right back down to the ground again. Reality hit me. Law and I being out here wasn't doing jack shit to keep her safe. These guys were definitely closing in on her. It was only a matter of time.

"Hey babe," I said, answering the phone, trying to catch my breath and sound cool. "Miss you."

"That's nice," she said. "We got a fucking situation back at the house. Ya'll probably need to drop whatever it is you're doing and get back here."

"What's wrong?" I asked, my mind immediately going to the worst possible place. "Are you alright?"

"I'm fine," she said. "For now. But I think shit's about to hit the fan."

# 31

## Athena

There was no way in hell I was going to get any sleep tonight, but it was easier pretending like I was tired and going to bed than having to sit out there in the barroom with Betty Sue.

Mama and I were having such a nice day. I could only hope when I was her age, I still had the kind of body she did, because she filled out a little black dress better than most women in their twenties. I straightened her hair and touched up her roots. I showed her how to do a smokey eye. We went out to the garage and she posed on the guys' motorcycles while I took pictures. The boys got a real kick out of it until Colt felt the need to spray them down with the hose.

When all was said and done, we didn't even end up using those pictures for her online dating profile. She didn't need all that to be a beautiful woman. I knew a lot about what kind of perverts lurked out there on the internet, and her straddling a motorcycle in a dress that barely covered her ass was probably the perfect bait for men like that. I convinced her to use one of her sitting in the sunshine on the front porch, her hair in a messy bun, her smile so big, there was no hiding the wrinkles around her eyes. To me, they were beautiful. To me, they showed a life of wisdom and experience, laughing and loving. The perfect man (or woman, I guess) would get it. And once they did, they would be given access to the super smutty pin up photos we took that day.

Tressica dropped by when she got off work, and the three of us laughed like no time had gone by, like we were just a bunch of lifelong friends trying to find a date for my mom. The guys really went above and beyond getting the clubhouse into a condition that would've made my daddy proud.

"Do you think the classy sluts will start coming around now?" Delaney asked.

"Dude, last I checked you were married," Miles said. "Don't be a fucking douche."

"So it's cool for Colt, but not for me. Gotcha." There was definitely some sort of weirdness going on between the two of them, but I brushed it off as a side effect of lockdown.

While they bickered about morals and ethics and marriage, Tressica and I interviewed my mom and got her set up with profiles on all the popular dating sites. It wasn't even five minutes before Judas' laptop started dinging and ringing. We passed a bottle of whiskey back and forth and laughed until we cried, ripping apart these poor fools, none of them even close to good enough for my beautiful mother. It helped keep my mind off of Judas and how worried I was about him. I knew he could take Harold with one hand tied behind his back, but shit was so complex right now. I prayed we weren't being set up. I trusted him and Law to take care of business, but they were going in blind. I almost felt guilty for enjoying the day with my mom, knowing that all this chaos was my own making.

In true Indignant fashion, things weren't quiet for long. My jaw nearly hit the floor when Betty Sue walked through the front door. She was wearing a giant sweatshirt that came down to her knees. She looked worse than she did the last time I saw her, like she'd been chained up, beaten, and starved.

Breaker and Rosey followed behind her. The way Breaker locked eyes with Colt sent a chill down my spine. My brother paced straight for the war room, and all the men followed behind without hesitation. I jumped up from my seat and chased after them, but the door slammed in my face and I heard the lock click immediately afterwards.

Soon Miles emerged from the room, slammed the door behind him, and ran for the front door at lightening speed.

"Where are you going?" I shouted after him. "What's going on?" He didn't even stop to acknowledge me. I looked at my mother in shock, and she just shrugged her shoulders. How could these women just keep their mouth shut when it was so obvious something was going down?

My brother stuck his head out of the war room. "What is happening?" I shouted.

"Tress," he said, looking over my shoulder. "Get in here?" She got up from the table and slinked past me, her head down. The door shut again, and I felt like I was being stabbed in the heart. Why wouldn't anyone tell me what was happening? Why were Betty Sue and Tressica allowed in the war room and I was stuck here outside in the dark? It wasn't fair. I felt like my chest was caving in and all the air was being sucked out of the room. I pounded on the door until my fists felt raw and bruised.

"Knock it the fuck off," Colt shouted from the other side, loud enough that I could hear. "You're not helping."

## Judas

"Let me in!" I screamed. "I know this has to do with me! You can't leave me out here in the dark."

He cracked the door open again. "Mama, you two go to the basement, please?"

I wedged my body between the door frame, refusing to move. "Why are you being so shady? Is Judas okay? What's *she* doing here?" I was spitting mad, my mind going in a million directions. Colt knew better than to treat me as some helpless damsel. I grew up in this life.

"Listen to me, Athena," he said, grabbing me by the shoulders. "Judas is fine. You're going to be fine. I'll be down to explain everything to you in a few minutes. I just need you to cooperate. Please?" His eyes were telling me a completely different story, but for some reason, in that instant, I felt like I needed to listen to him. It wasn't because he reminded me of my father. My father was never this composed in times of trouble. I nodded, and he wrapped his arms around me in a warm embrace. "It's going to be alright."

Down to the basement Reena and I went. We sat there in the darkness passing a joint back and forth, not saying a word, every creak in the floorboard damn near sending me leaping for the ceiling.

"I'm so sorry," I finally whispered, tears running from my eyes. She wrapped her arm around me and brushed her fingers through my hair. For the first time in my life, I understood the comfort of a mother's love.

## 32

## Judas

I hopped the first flight back to Pittsburgh I could catch. Law and Sabrina were driving back. She had no ID, no passport, nothing but the nightgown on her back, and there was no way in hell we'd be able to get her on a plane without some serious string pulling. For all I knew she was a minor, a missing person, and taking her across state lines would land our asses in jail. I didn't have time for all that. My club was about to be under attack. My woman was on the line here. My brother was the one who put the wheels in motion.

This was all my fault.

It was four in the morning but I was more wide awake than I'd felt in a long time. Fight, flight, fuck, I was ready to go, flying down the back roads through the mountains on my motorcycle in pitch darkness. I wasn't going to sleep until I knew Athena was safe, and once we took care of this situation, I was never going to let her out of my sight again.

I stopped at a gas station to fill up and check my phone. I called Colt first, hoping Athena wasn't too far

## Judas

away. They had found Isaac a few hours earlier and took him out to the warehouse, thinking they could use him as bait. The clubhouse was in full on lockdown mode, windows boarded up, everyone on high alert. Nobody was sleeping tonight. Everyone was armed and ready for anything.

Everyone but me. I felt so fucking helpless, even though at this rate I'd be home in less than an hour. "Where's Athena?" I asked.

"She's in your room. Rosey's sitting outside the door. She's fine. Mad as hell, but fine. Betty Sue on the other hand... she's a fucking mess."

"I don't care," I said. "Bitch is as much to blame." I hadn't got the whole story, but I knew her and Isaac were in this together. She'd been mistaking my kindness for weakness this whole time, seeing just how far she could push me. She had been making a fool out of me and I just let her. That ended today. "I'll see ya in an hour," I said, mounting my bike for the last leg of my journey.

I hadn't seen the clubhouse on lockdown like this in a long time, not since we were young bucks. Q-Tip had a taste for the kind of trouble that made us hide out for days on end, waiting for the enemy to strike. Felt kinda like the good old days. Maybe they were the 'bad old days.' It tied my stomach in knots thinking about what this sight actually entailed. The windows were boarded up, and Sharky and Delaney sat outside the front gate in the parking lot. They unlocked the wire fence for me and waved me in.

"Ya'll got everything you need out here?" I asked. "I'll be out in a minute to relieve you."

"Go get some rest, man," Delaney said. That wasn't going to happen.

Not tonight.

Not ever. Not until I knew my girl was safe to walk down the street in broad daylight.

If these motherfuckers were going to try and attack the club, I wanted my smiling face to be the first thing they saw.

It smelled like denial and Pine-sol in the barroom. I screwed the plywood back on the door behind me with the power drill sitting on the pool table. Nobody said anything, everyone half drunk, half high. Everyone pretending like tonight was business as usual, even though we had no idea what was going to happen from one minute to the next. Each of the big screen TVs on the walls were connected to a different surveillance camera so we could see everything going on outside of the building. One TV was split into a bunch of smaller squares, each showing a different room of the warehouse. In the bottom corner of the screen, Isaac sat on a metal folding chair, arms and legs bound. I couldn't tell if he was sleeping or knocked out. I didn't give a fuck.

Betty Sue reached for my arm. I clenched my fist, feeling the rage welling up inside of me.

"Don't ever touch me again," I growled.

"Judas, I was the one that stopped him from kidnapping her!" she pleaded. "You can't be mad at me. That Isaac thing, I was just trying to get your attention."

"You had my attention for years. I wanted nothing more than to see you get well, even after we broke up. I'm done with your shit. You were never good enough for me, woman. You and Isaac are a match made in heaven. Knowing you, you probably had something to do with all this shit."

"Fuck you," she muttered, lighting up a cigarette, blowing a mouthful of smoke right in my face. "Have fun

## Judas

playing house with your whore. I'm sure she'll get tired of your shit real quick."

"Banished," I said, shrugging my shoulders. "Your ass is banished from this place."

"We'll see about that," she said, rolling her eyes. Colt was already unscrewing the door.

"Can I get my shoes back?" Tressica asked, a sly grin on her face. "They're kind of my favorites."

"I'll bring em to your place tomorrow." Tressica held out her hand, shaking her head.

"You're banished, bitch. You've been fucking with my boy for way too long. Now you're trying to fuck with my girl? Shoes!" she demanded. I guess I could've stuck around and watched them scrap it out, but I'd already wasted enough time. I needed to see Athena. I knew the boys were keeping her safe, but I needed her now.

I stormed down the hallway and Rosey jumped to alert. His bloodshot eyes let me know he needed sleep. "Get out of here," I said. "Go take a load off. Thanks for looking out for my woman." I patted him on the shoulder and he smiled at me with his goofy ass grin.

"If anything ever happens to you, I'll make damn sure she's well taken care of."

"Go away you sick fuck," I growled, pointing down the hallway. He wrapped his arms around me in a brotherly hug.

"Everything is gonna be alright," he said. "I got your back, Jude."

I unlocked the bedroom door and heard her gasp. I flicked on the light and she sat upright in the bed, clutching her pistol in her hand. "It's okay," I whispered. "It's just me."

She charged across the room like a possessed woman,

dropping her gun to the floor. She jumped into my arms and started mauling me with her mouth like a wild cheetah, kissing me in that needy kinda way that made my dick rock hard and my heart race. I cupped her perfect ass and kissed her back, our tongues dancing as we both struggled to breathe.

"I need you to love me right now," she whispered. "I need you, Judas."

"I love you all the time, baby doll," I said. "You know that."

"I need you inside me," she cried out.

I needed to be inside her as much as she needed me. All the heaviness, all the drama, all the uncertainty, the only thing that could wash away my sins was in between my woman's legs.

I pressed her back against the wall and unzipped my jeans, pulling out my cock. I dragged my tongue down her neck until she screamed, pulling her panties down around her knees and thrusting into her without a word, stretching her warm wet cunt around me, the groans in the back of her throat a mix of pleasure and pain. She dug her fingernails into my shoulders and it just drove me to fuck her harder.

I thrust into her with all my might, her eyes rolling back in her head.

"Yes," she moaned. "Take it all out on me, baby. Use me, Judas." I reached for her clit, desperate to feel her walls shatter around me, desperate to see her lose control. It made me feel so powerful knowing I could manipulate her body in the same way she manipulated my soul. The deeper I drove inside of her, the deeper I felt her inside of me, saving my soul, making me whole again.

I felt her shatter, her legs growing stiff and her moans escalating, and I filled her with my seed, unable to hold off any longer. She pressed her head to my chest and sighed. I carried her to the bed and set her down, lovingly tussling her hair, kissing on her forehead. I wanted to stay.

I needed to go.

I needed to go keep my promise to her.

She pouted as I walked away, stripped out of my clothes and tossed them in the hamper. She followed me into the bathroom and watched my every move as I stepped into the shower. Harold's blood washed from my skin down the drain, tinting the water red.

"Judas," she stammered. "What is that?"

"It's your freedom, babe." I hurriedly cleaned myself up, toweled myself off, and dressed, and she didn't once let me out of her sight.

"I don't like this. I'm scared," she said as I slid back into my boots. I kissed her on the forehead. She wasn't an idiot. She had every right to be scared. I had no idea what the next twenty four hours were going to bring. I had no idea what it was going to take to make everything alright. All I knew is that whatever it took was going to be worth it. Worth more than anything I'd ever done in my life. She was my woman now, and I would kill to make sure she never had to be sad or scared ever again.

"Relax, baby," I said. "Trust me."

"Can't you just stay a little?" she pleaded. "Can't we take care of it in the morning?"

She was smiling sadly, like she already knew the answer to her question. I ran my fingers through her hair, studied her face a little longer than I should've, kissed her lips a little harder than I needed to.

"I'll be back soon," I said. "Be good. I love you."

"You better promise me," she said.

"Every word that comes out of my mouth is a promise to you, Athena. Know that on my life."

## 33

## Judas

"Who the fuck were you talking to?" I shouted, slamming the pipe wrench off my brother's shin. The guys had already worked him over pretty good. His eyes were black, a circle of dried blood around his nose and mouth, and the second I hit him with the wrench, he started to throw up. "Isaac, come on! Man the fuck up."

"I don't know!" he said. "Honest! They call me from a different number every time."

He looked so pathetic sitting there. I *felt* so pathetic beating on him while he was tied up and helpless, but I had to take a step back from who he was and what I was doing to him and focus on the matter at hand. This asshole, this person I shared a womb with for nine months inside of my mother, he wasn't my family anymore. He was trying to ruin my family. The MC were the only people in this world who mattered to me, and Athena was the only woman I ever really loved.

I swung back the wrench, getting ready to pop him in the other shin but my conscience got the best of me. This wasn't making me feel better. This wasn't getting us anywhere.

I dropped the wrench to the ground and he breathed out a loud sigh of relief.

"Why did you do it, Isaac? I've been so fucking good to you. I took you in when you had nobody. I brought you into my crew." My voice was wavering. I slapped my hands over my face and screamed.

"Only reason why you took me in was so that ya'll could make a fool of me. You knew I'd never get patched in. You set me up for failure."

"You set yourself up for failure, you pussy," Colt shouted. "You of all people should know your brother ain't a hurtful guy. He brought you in 'cuz you're supposed to be his kin. He treated you better than your ass deserved."

Isaac's laugh echoed through the concrete building. He'd lost his damn mind.

"That's right. Can't forget Judas can do no wrong. You were always the golden child, no matter what you did. Even after I got your ass locked up, you came out smelling like a rose. I'm sick of living in your fucking shadow."

Colt picked up the wrench from the floor and bashed him across the face. The sound of teeth hitting the concrete reminded me of the first day I met Colt on the school bus. He knew that day we were going to be best friends for life. He knew all along that Isaac was nothing but trouble, but he loved me enough to respect my wishful thinking.

"Sorry," Colt said, handing me the wrench. "It's been a long day. I'll be good now."

"Where's your phone?" I asked Isaac. That was the only hold up. We needed to get these people on the phone. We needed Isaac to get them here. I knew jack shit about the Russian Mafia, and I had no idea what kind of firepower they were going to show up with, but I'd rather it go down at the warehouse than back at the clubhouse.

"I don't know!" he shouted, blood pouring from his mouth. "I swear."

"Got it," Breaker said, peeking his head around the corner. "Well hot damn!" His eyes grew wide when he caught sight of Isaac. The kid was a scrapper. Reena might've called him heartbreaker, the girls called him jawbreaker, but when Colt found him on the street and brought him into the club it was because he watched him beat down a bunch of thugs on Main Street in broad daylight. "*He broke their fucking faces!*" Colt had exclaimed to us all.

"You want some of that?" Colt asked. "Got him warmed up for ya."

"Maybe later," Breaker said. "I like em better when they can fight back." He got right up in Isaac's face and barked and Isaac damn near fell over backwards, taking the chair he was tied up in with him.

"It didn't have to be like this, Ike," Colt teased. "You could've just kept your nose down and been a good little prospect."

"Just kill me now," he pleaded. "I know you're going to anyway."

The phone in Breaker's hand started to ring. My blood started pumping. That could be them.

"You wanna live or you wanna die?" I asked him. "Choice is up to you. Answer this call, tell em you got her, and give them the details, or I'll throw you to Moses chair and all."

"How do I know you're telling the truth?" he asked.

"You really don't know me at all, do you brother?"

"This motherfucker never lies," Colt said.

## 34

## Judas

Now all we had to do was wait. Colt, Breaker, Miles, and I hid in the office watching the surveillance cameras. It was damn near two in the afternoon, and we were all a little more than on edge, tired, hungry, ready for action. The Russians were on the way to the warehouse. Under normal circumstances, we could just make them disappear. This wasn't normal circumstances. We needed this problem gone for good.

I had the backpack full of cash Athena showed up with initially. We had a pile of guns, a pile of coke, a shit load of property at our disposal. Killing everyone and going about our lives wasn't an option. We had to use more than just our muscles to smooth things over with the enemy.

A black SUV pulled into the parking lot. Two short bald men climbed out of the back.

"We could totally take em," Colt said.

"You know these goons are just the tip of the iceberg," I reminded him. "I don't feel like playing whack a mole for the rest of my life."

The man who stepped out of the passenger side was

taller than a giant and wider than a tree. He had a scar on his forehead that looked like he'd been scalped at some point in his life. It's very rare I found myself intimidated by another man based on their appearance alone. This motherfucker looked like he could take a full round to the gut and keep on swinging. His three piece suit probably cost more than my motorcycle, only adding to my apprehension. These men just weren't in it for the money.

"They're coming in," Breaker said. "That's my cue." He slipped out the back door and into the darkness.

"Oh, Isaac," the man called out in a thick Russian accent, his voice echoing through the warehouse. "Where are you, my friend?"

The men split up, exploring the building, calling for Isaac, calling for Athena. Every time I heard her name on the men's lips, my stomach stirred. I tried not to think of what they planned on doing with my woman, or else I would've completely lost it and just gone out guns blazing.

One of the smaller men finally stepped into the murder room, shouting in rage when he got a look at Isaac sitting there, tied to the chair, bleeding from his mouth and half unconscious. "What the fuck!?" he shouted.

The other two quickly joined him. I rushed out into the hallway and slammed the door behind them, triple checking it was locked.

"What the fuck!" the giant man screamed, pounding his fists on the stainless steel door, denting it a little bit with every blow until his fists were bloodied.

"I'm gonna need everybody to calm down," Colt said over the intercom. He started to chuckle as we watched the three of them look up at the ceiling and begin cursing.

"Show your face!" he screamed. "Fucking pussy!"

They began to turn the room upside down, smashing

# Judas

shelves to the floor, kicking the doors, going completely wild like a bunch of caged animals.

"Think they're gonna tire themselves out?" Miles asked.

"Who did this to you?" one of them screamed in Isaac's face. "Where did they take her?" All three of them had their guns drawn at this point. The one caught sight of the emergency exit, beckoning for the other two to join him. They trained their guns at the door, and he pushed on the bar to open it, peeking his head into Moses' new home.

"What the hell is that?" the one screamed, immediately slamming the door again. The other one looked, and shut the door, too.

"Fuckin' shoot it," the giant shouted.

"Don't even think about it," Colt said over the intercom. "Moses eats bullets for breakfast. It's lunch time now. He's probably in the mood for some cabbage and vodka."

"You racist fuck," the bald guy shouted, waving his fist in the air. Colt was chuckling like a son of a bitch, a little too impressed with himself. "Come out here and show your face! Be a man!"

One of the guys took to slapping Isaac in the face and screaming at him. While amusing, it wasn't really productive. "What are you trying to do there, fella?" Colt asked. "Settle down. Drop your guns. We just want to talk to you."

"Where's the bitch?" the tallest shouted.

"I think I'm looking at him," Colt chuckled. I ripped the speaker out of his hand.

"We just want to talk to you," I said. "I think we can work something out that'll make everybody happy. Look under the chair." He eyed the ceiling quizzically, looking like he was mulling over in his head whether or not he was being set up. "Just do it."

As he unzipped Athena's backpack, his eyes lit up for a second. He slid the stacks of cash around.

"That's all your money, and then some."

"Oh that's cute," he finally said. "You think this about money? This shit is personal."

"Way I see it is, you got two options. We can make a deal and everybody walks outta here alive, or I can leave ya'll here to rot. You think your boss wants to find out you got set up by a bunch of scumbag bikers? Over some fucking bitch?" I cringed when I said those words. It was a struggle separating myself from who I needed to be right now and how I really felt, but the more I downplayed how insignificant she was, the more likely I was to get what I wanted from these fuckers. "She made a mistake. She obviously fucked with the wrong guys. Now that you're here, though, I got a proposition for you. You might not know about the Indignant Few, but we're some smart motherfuckers as you can see. You want protection? You want to expand your business? You want all access to this place? We have guns. We have cash. We have drugs. We have everything you need to set up shop."

"Like an alliance?" he asked.

"Get your boss on the phone. We can make friends, or we can make war for the rest of our fucking lives. Choice is up to you."

The Indignants didn't make deals with the devil, but for Athena, I would sell my soul to anybody who asked. Keeping our enemies close was going to have to be the temporary band-aid on this bleeding wound.

Besides, it was only temporary. I had an ace up my sleeve in the form of a fifteen year old broad named Sabrina who had names, faces, and was ready to sing like a bird. Law had the connections to make sure none of these

## Judas

guys ever saw the outside world ever again. They didn't know those wheels were in motion.

*Live for the moment,* she'd said to me, that first night we hooked up.

*I don't want anybody to get hurt,* she'd said, pleading with me to let her turn herself into the authorities.

*Trust me,* I'd said all along, not even knowing at that point how I was going to make this right. In the end, I got to be the man I wanted to be. She got her freedom. She might have sacrificed years of her life to that scumbag Harold, but now, she was saving another woman from the same fate. She was saving a lot of women from being bought and sold. She was bringing down a dangerous crime organization, and she didn't even know it. Fate had been good to both of us.

"He wants a sit down," the ogre said, hanging up his phone. "Where's the closest airport to this shit hole."

We all walked out into the parking lot, unscathed. Well, almost all of us. We offered them Isaac as collateral, but their opinion on traitors was about the same as ours.

"Tell me you're sorry," I said as I untied him from the chair.

"Fuck you," he muttered. "I'll see you in hell."

Maybe he would, but I didn't care. Right now, I had heaven on earth. I'd reached a state of nirvana. My real family was safe. My woman never had to worry another day in her life. I was standing on the edge of my future, and for the first time, it looked like I was going to get to live the life of my dreams.

I jumped a little when I heard the gun go off as I walked out of the building. I could only hope he'd finally found his peace. Maybe I wasn't the best brother to him, but maybe by bringing him here, I did the best I could do to protect the rest of the world from his anger.

"Come on, Breaker," I said through the rolled down window of the SUV. He was sitting in the passenger seat, passing a joint back and forth with the Russian driver. They looked like they were getting along like long lost friends. He was such a fucking enigma. When he wasn't smashing faces in, he was a sneaky motherfucker, everybody's best buddy. He could charm the pants off just about anyone, including the Russian Mafia.

"It was nice meeting ya, Hedeon," he said. "I got some real good shit back at the house. Stop by sometime and I'll hook you up."

"Don't get too attached," I muttered under my breath. He shot me a wink.

We watched as they drove off and then mounted our bikes.

"What the fuck did we just do?" Colt stammered. "Fuckin' Athena. She's always been a pain in my dick." I laughed as I drove off, speeding ahead. Fucking Athena was what I was about to be doing. On the bed. In the shower. In our new farm house. Filling her with babies. Making her the happiest woman alive. Fuckin' Athena. She'd always been a pain in my dick, too.

## 35

## Athena

"Little nervous?" I asked Judas, watching him fumble trying to tap the keg of beer. We were all on high alert. It wasn't every day we invited the FBI to a rally. We were throwing the Russian Mafia a welcome to America party they'd never forget. Brother chapters of the Indignants from all over the state were piling into the parking lot of the clubhouse on their bikes. The band had already started, and Delaney and his wife Pearline were working the BBQ pit, the smell of charcoal drifting through the air.

It felt good seeing everybody come together to celebrate after a heavy fucking lockdown and a few weeks of playing nice with the mob and trying to lay low. It felt good that I could finally be outside in the sunshine with my man, holding his hand, hanging out with our crew without worrying about having a target on my back.

"I wish I would've got you a leash," he said, laughing nervously. "You know I'm going to freak out if I lose sight of you for a second."

"Leashes are for the bedroom," I teased. "Besides, it's gonna be alright. I hope these motherfuckers are worse at spotting cops than I am, though." It did make me uncomfortable knowing that the very men who were trying to kidnap me were currently rubbing elbows with the rest of the crew, but I put on a brave face, making jokes about how they took my life's savings away. They were amused enough to irritate me, but hell, I'd give them every dime I made for the next fifty years if it meant my family would be safe.

We weren't just doing this for ourselves, anyway. The second I met Sabrina, I felt like I was looking into a mirror of a younger version of myself. When I found out what the mafia did to her parents after they took her and sold her, I knew we had to do whatever it took to get these assholes behind bars. She was staying at a safe house for the time being, but I knew the club was the safest place for her to be. I was going to make sure she never went down the same path I did. I was going to make sure her life had a happily ever after much faster than I got my own. It was the least I could do for sitting on my hands for so long, watching Harold exploit girls to line his pockets.

"Ready to go to jail, bud?" Judas asked Law, handing him a freshly poured beer. He chugged it down and refilled his cup.

"Wouldn't be the first time," Law said with a laugh. "I figure if I get myself liquored up enough it'll be an exciting challenge." I didn't know what kind of strings he had to pull, hell, I didn't even know who he worked for, but I did know he was getting arrested along side the Russians today. I also knew he was going to be out by tomorrow morning. Hopefully by then, there'd still be cold beer, loud music, and a couple of hot sluts waiting to give him a welcome home present. He'd definitely earned it.

Judas slid his hand into the back pocket of my shorts as we walked through the crowd. I was starting to like this old lady shit. He was as much my property as I was his. I was so proud of him and everything he did to defend our lifestyle. I had myself a trophy boyfriend, and I knew all the women here were dripping with jealousy just by the way they sneered at me. I finally had it made, and all it took was a life of pornography, ripping off the Russian mafia, and a few months of fearing for my life. Totally worth it.

I was home.

Zelda was clinging to my brother like a spider monkey, a little bit drunker and louder than I'd ever seen her, and I tried to keep Tressica entertained. It pained me to see my best friend so sad, even though she made this bed for herself by hopping into bed with my brother. Colt never took his eyes off her, and I didn't know if it made things better or worse. All I could do was feed her shots and crack jokes. She could have any man she wanted in this crowd. It hurt my heart knowing she only wanted the one who she could never fully have.

We sat on a picnic table, picking at a pile of ribs while Judas chomped down on a veggie burger and and Law slammed down a bottle of Jameson.

"I think I'm gonna go," Tress said. Zelda was standing on top of a speaker, her shirt up over her head, laughing loud enough you could only hear her voice over the music and the crowd. "I can't watch this anymore."

"No way," Judas said. "You're one of us. You gotta stick around for the fireworks."

And that's when the magic happened. Flashing lights. Megaphones. Swat teams. Shots fired. Law finished the bottle of whiskey and shot us a wink as he walked away, his hands in the air. We sat there and watched the chaos, just staring out into the crowd as men were tackled to the ground. Judas clutched my hand, and I smiled, everything moving in slow motion. Our entire biker family did the same. They knew what was happening. A round of applause rang through the air, and everyone stepped out of the way, letting the police and FBI do their business.

I felt like a pile of bricks had been lifted from my shoulders. Judas pressed his lips to mine, and I knew he felt the same. This was what freedom felt like - freedom to be the person I was always meant to be. Freedom to love the man I was fated to spend the rest of my life with.

No more running from my destiny. No more hiding out. This was exactly where I belonged.

## 36

## Epilogue: ONE YEAR LATER: Athena

Well that was a sight I'd never grow tired of. I watched from the kitchen window, sipping my tea. Judas was slamming his hoe into the dirty field, shirt off, sweat pouring down his abs, his perfect biceps rippling with every strike. It was taking everything in me not to tackle him to the earth, roll around in the dirt with him until we were both caked in mud.

It was gonna have to wait.

I opened the window and shouted out to him, "Hey love, you're going to have to put a shirt on soon. I have clients coming, and I don't need 'em getting all riled up."

"I thought we were going to the dam today," he shouted back. He looked a little disappointed, so I opened up my bathrobe and flashed him through the screen.

"Later," I said. "Gotta feed the wedding fund first."

"You better put those titties away, then. You're making me hungry."

I blew him a kiss and rushed to our bedroom to finish getting ready for the day. I slid into a chambray sundress, flopped a straw hat on my head, and dabbed some sunscreen on my face. I liked this 'around the house' look. Nobody gave a shit if my nails had dirt under them or I put on a couple pounds. I didn't care what anybody thought anyway. The only person who mattered was currently stripping down to nothing in the master bathroom. I licked my lips and admired his hot body, tanned from spending time out in the field.

"Who you getting all clean for?" I asked as he started running the shower. "You know I like you dirty." I pecked him on the lips and tried to fight the sensation between my legs.

"Fuckin' Breaker," he muttered. "Shit's going down at Zelda's house and I gotta go help him out."

"Where's Colt?" I asked. He shrugged and pecked me on the lips. I could tell he wasn't too thrilled.

"Ugh," I said. "You know how I always said I wanted you to tell me everything? Keep me outta that one, please."

"You and me, both," he said, stepping into the shower.

I heard the sound of tires in our dirt driveway and looked out the bedroom window. A red convertible full of white haired old ladies parked in front of the house. They were laughing and singing along to the radio. These were my favorite kinds of clients. It brought a smile to my face.

"I gotta go, babe," I said, opening up the shower door and smacking his round wet ass.

"Have fun making your old lady porn," he teased.

"You have fun dealing with crazy and the crew. What do you want to get into tonight?"

"Oh, you know exactly what I want to get into. You sure you don't have time for a quickie?"

"Listen, these chicks' clocks are ticking," I said with a giggle. "I'll see you tonight. I love you." He stuck his head

## Judas

out of the shower and kissed me on the lips, electric sparks filling my body as always. Was it normal to have a massive crush on your fiancé? Everything about him still turned me into a puddle of goo. I skipped off, my face beet red and my heart racing.

"Hey girls!" I shouted, stepping out onto the front porch. "You ready to have some fun?"

I walked them to the garage out back and cracked open a bottle of wine.

"Bernie is going to shit himself," the woman named Ruby said as I took her hair down from the sloppy bun and began to work some mousse through it.

"Bernie shits himself anyway," her friend Rose teased.

"At least I got a man," Ruby said, cackling with laughter.

"Well, I promise, once I'm done with you Rose, you will have men lining up outside your door."

I wasn't in the porn business per se, even though I did boudoir photography. I was in the business of empowering women. All women, no matter how old they were deserved to feel sexy. Here in the barn, I fixed their hair and make-up, let them pick out sexy outfits, and took flattering photographs of them. It was a lot of fun, not just for me, but for my clients, too. Maybe I wasn't blessed with a lot of natural talents, but I'd finally learned how to put the ones I had to good use. I knew how to make people feel sexy. I knew how to make people feel wanted.

Seeing the smiles on my clients faces as they walked out the door with a disk of dirty pictures of themselves brought me a sense of accomplishment I never felt before, even when I was running my other business. I got to do something I loved, and give back to the community.

"You ladies are free to pick out some clothes while I

finish Ruby's hair," I said. "Help yourself to the wine. My fiancé made you some snacks." I motioned to the table Judas had set up for us. It was so sweet the way he supported my business. The ladies seemed to appreciate it, too.

"Your fiancé *is* a snack," Rose said. "I wouldn't mind riding him like a Harley."

I cracked up. "Don't make me fight you, Rose. I know you're single and on the prowl."

"You blow your back out getting into the car," Ruby snapped at her. "A man like that would put you in the nursing home for good."

Rose held up a red g-string with a beaded butterfly that sat right on the ass crack. "You're probably right. I'd break a hip trying to get into this thing. I think I'm just gonna go au natural. You know once you get a certain age, you stop growing hair down there."

"Oh dear lord," I said, slapping my hand over my mouth.

My heart was exploding with joy. My life was absolutely perfect.

"Aren't you gonna have some wine, too?" Ruby asked as I took a curling iron and began to wrap it around her bangs.

I shook my head and smiled, placing my hand over my stomach. "Don't tell anybody," I said with a wink.

"How exciting!" she squealed. "You're blessed!"

I was so fucking blessed, and soon, we would welcome a new life into this world and show him or her what heaven on earth really was. Our love for each other would inspire a new generation, a generation who would never have to see the things we saw, or feel our pains. Judas and I, we were going to build the future of the Indignant Few MC.

## Judas

Judas and I, our love alone was enough to fulfill our ultimate purpose.

THE END

Thank you for Reading!

I hope you loved Judas as much as I loved writing about him and the rest of the crew. I'd love to hear your thoughts!

To stay up to date on my future releases, including Breaker's story in Book 2 of the Indignant Few MC, please feel free to hop on my mailing list here, or follow me on social below! (I promise I will never spam you, but I might send you a couple steamy bonus chapters here and there!)

**To learn about my past releases, including the Mountain Misfits MC, now available in a complete box set, check out my Amazon author page!**

Made in the USA
Coppell, TX
19 April 2023

15789177R00135